THE LYCANTHROPES DIARY

Volume I: Sons and Sisters

By: R. S. Wells

Dedication

This book is dedicated to my friends and family, both living and dead.

My wonderful wife Judy, without whom this book would never be made public. I don't do legalese and red tape very well. She does.

My friends Mike and Crystal Dumas and their two lads, who always have been in my corner no matter what.

My friends Steve Kwiatkowski and Elizabeth (Barnes) MacDougal who have spent many hours trying to keep me sane over the years. I'm not saying that they succeeded, just that they tried. ☺

And to the loving memory of my sister in law Heather who recently passed from brain cancer, taken far before her time, as well as to the memory of my best friend Bill Wedge, (Urs), who died in 2005 at the young age of 29. He helped me work on this series concept over many cans of beer and shots of whiskey. You're both loved and greatly missed.

And finally, to the good folks at KDP for making this real.

I thank you all.

Contents

Chapter One

Derrek

Derrek swam around for almost an hour, just marveling at the ancient temple. It was Egyptian originally, dedicated to the God of wisdom Thoth, but it wasn't Egyptian artifacts that he and the team were after. He checked his tank for air, then went over to the small group of archaeologists that he was assisting and clicked his headset on so that he could communicate with them.

"This temple is almost another five hundred years older than previous ones we've found. There is evidence of early Son activity, and possibly even O'Sian." Dr. Wedge told them as he pointed to a hieroglyph. Derrek nodded along with the others and then made a mental note to thank his Allied contact back in Eastern Canada for helping him get this job.

He was a seventh-generation Ally, and his family had served the Sons of Lycaon loyally. Now, he was the first of his family to be able to actually be involved with the SERIOUS Son business, not just going around delivering messages and cleaning up tracks. The Sons trusted no one until they had proved themselves over several generations. As a seventh-generation Ally, Derrek was now able to learn more about the Son's history, like how they were created by aliens and that they were what humans referred to as werewolves.

Derrek had to pinch himself from time to time to realize that he wasn't dreaming. A week ago, he was just a barber in a small town. Now, here he was, scuba diving off the Egyptian coast, working on a secret archaeological dig. This was huge to him.

"The O'Sian's were aliens from long ago that had come to Earth. They weren't the first ones to come to Earth; according to our records, our world and our very genes have been played with by other extra-terrestrial visitors before." Dr. Wedge said over the headset. His voice sounded funny over the headset, all of their voices did, like they were speaking with a plugged nose.

One of the other researchers spoke up then, another guy with a stream of letters after his name. Derrek was the only one in the group without an advanced degree, assuming his barber certification didn't count. "So how many races have worked on us?" the other scientist asked Dr. Wedge.

"We are sure of at least eight, to lesser and greater degrees, but it was mostly the O'Sian's, Nom'I'Kon, and the "Others." These "Others" seemed to be a unified collective of dozens of genetically similar races. We know the "O'Sian's" and the "Others" were bipedal and had some similar organs, albeit the O'Sian's were over double our height tall and covered in fur with snouts and claws, but the Nom'I'Kon were more bat-like, able to fly and they survived by ingesting the blood of animals. They didn't have arms per se, and they did not use technology. It is a mystery why they were even taken here at all. The "Others" seem to be related to the "Grey Aliens" you commonly hear about. Smaller, no hair, big black eyes. Actually, they are part of a huge group of related races." Dr. Wedge told the group and Derrek could hear the others murmuring in agreement.

"So, were the Nom'I'Kon the basis of the vampires we have now?" one of the other researchers asked and Derrek was glad because he was wondering the same thing but was scared to speak up.

"Yes. There are four shape-shifting species on Earth. But the main two are from the O'Sian and the Nom'I'Kon races. There are far more vampires than there are Sons of Lycaon, but the Sons are far more powerful," the old doctor answered. There was a slight pause for the information to sink in and then Dr. Wedge spoke again.

"These four shape-shifting races were somehow able to cross the astral plane into our realm and travel back and forth. All of the species that were created served a purpose. Humans were to be the builders and caretakers of the world. The bulk of the labor force and population. The shape-shifting races were initially considered to be a mistake and were set to be annihilated until the master races seen that they could both harness astral energy to travel between two realms. And since the master race's primary interests was astral energy… they decided that the shifter races were worthy of study. There are rumors that these ancient shifting races were originally huge, O'Sian sized, and that they are considered to be the giants mentioned in the Bible. They were later manipulated to be smaller."

One of the other researchers spoke up then. "Astral realms are stacked together, are they not? Like pages in a book? Each is another plane of existence, and each with slightly different vibrational energies. Completely other realms. And since each realm has slightly different energies, astral energy from other realms that came here to ours could be used to violate the laws of physics in this realm… In some cases, making the impossible possible. Am I correct?"

Dr. Wedge nodded, leaving a wiggling trail of bubbles as he did. "Correct, Dr. Barnes. Over time, it was discovered that by using selective breeding, they were able to create human families that had stronger ties to the astral realms, allowing more and more energy to come in to our realm from the other realm, enabling the Son to swap places with these humans and travel from their astral realm to our physical realm. They were able to get their mitochondria, which as you all know, are the powerhouse of the cells, to draw astral energy and use it to change forms. Changing form was basically reversing existences… Flipping beings from one realm to the other."

Derrek followed the doctor and the others as they went into

the temple complex itself. The walls were bare of hieroglyphs inside, which surprised him a bit, but as they swam through the ancient water-filled corridors, they began to see different-looking symbols carved on the walls. O'Sian glyphs. He recognized them by their look, but he didn't know what any of them meant.

"We see here that the glyphs are no longer Egyptian, but O'Sian. We'll need to document everything we can and then destroy it before non-Allied teams find it. Shame though. I do hate destroying history." Dr. Wedge told them as they came to a stop in a chamber.

Derrek went along with the others, photographing every O'Sian glyph carved into the walls before then erasing them with a laser-like tool the Son council of the Alliance had sent along with them. It basically worked like an eraser, leaving behind the smooth stone where the carved stone once was. He had been at it for several minutes when his headset clicked on and Dr. Wedge's voice came on, speaking in an excited tone.

"We've found something! We've found something! Some type of artifact that seems to have been designed for drawing astral power! It's obviously O'Sian, not even of this realm! I can sense it still works… It seems to be tugging at me… And I can feel other energy flowing into it from elsewhere. We need to take this to the Council laboratory at once!"

The doctor picked up the object and placed it in a small sack. He then radioed to the surface. He tried two more times before looking at the others with a confused sort of look on his face through his swim mask.

"Odd. The boats are not responding. It must be some type of interference from the artifact. Derrek, you're the youngest and most athletic of the group, take the artifact up to the boat, will you?" the doctor told him and then handed him the sack.

"Yes, Doctor Wedge," Derrek replied, his tone eager. Dr. Wedge was a thirty-second generational ally, trusted with knowledge Derrek could only hope to guess at. With time came the rewards… and the Son's didn't trust much information to the lower generations of Allies.

Derrek was halfway to the surface when he has seen the other boat parked next to theirs. In the distance, he could see other bodies in the water, swimming down towards the temple.

"The Alliance must have sent another boat," he thought and then leisurely made his way towards the smaller of the boats stopped above him.

He broke the surface and gasped in shock. The crew of the small boat that had taken them out to the site was dead. The body of one of the crew was half hanging over the side, his neck sliced wide, but no blood was to be seen.

"Vampires!" Derrek gasped to himself and then looked around the water near him for any signs that he had been seen. The vampires normally wouldn't dare bother with the Alliance. The Grand Alliance of the Sons was feared and powerful. The lowest Son was worth more than the highest Vampire, it was written in the ancient texts and the vampires knew it as well as the Son's did. For them to try something this risky… It had to be important.

Derrek heard a screechy sound and turned to see someone pointing at him while another person aimed a rifle. Derrek gulped air and dove, not even putting his snorkel back in, and heard the low thrum of an automatic rifle firing into the water near him. Sharp little plucking sounds came from the bullets as they slammed into the water, but he was soon down and out of their reach.

He swam then. He swam like a madman for the shore… Several miles away. He swam like his life depended on it, which it did. He swam like he was on a mission, which he was. He swam until he was nearly to the point of passing out from exhaustion, then he forced himself past it and swam some more.

He knew the others were dead. There was no sense going back to look. He knew that the vampires would likely have someone on shore waiting to kill him and take the artifact from him. He knew he was deep over his head and not just in water. He had to get the artifact to safety… To the Son Council, or at least to someone

Allied.

****

Derrek finally made it to shore at night time. He had been hiding four hours in the rough surf from three armed men that he seen walking the beach. His air tank was now out, and he was unarmed except for a diving knife. He knew he had to wait them out rather than fight them because he could tell that the three men were vampires. They were dressed in black Arabic attire, like most of the locals, but unlike the locals, these three men were carrying submachine guns on slings over their shoulders.

The men gave up at last, and Derrek waited another half hour in the pounding waves before he finally crept to shore. The first thing he did was make his way to a corner store where he put the artifact into a box and had it mailed to his Allied contact, with a note telling him to get it to the Son Council. He didn't have any money on him, so he exchanged the delivery for his air tanks and divers knife.

He left the store and persuaded the small taxi to take him to his hotel in exchange for his diving flippers. He drew some strange looks going through the lobby in a wet suit, but the concierge identified him and unlocked his room's door for him.

Derrek thanked the man and closed the door to his room and flicked on the light. He had to call someone and let them know, but the only one he could think of in the immediate area was the likely deceased Dr. Wedge.

He thought for a moment and then snapped his fingers. He picked up the phone and made a collect call to a number of a known Grand Alliance contact and was waiting for the long distance operator to connect him when he heard a sudden movement come towards him from his bathroom.

He turned just in time to get a glimpse of a white-haired older Arabic man in their traditional robes rushing toward him, then he felt a sharp pain in his abdomen. He gasped and felt the energy draining from him. He grabbed at the man, but only wound up gripping onto his robes. The man withdrew the knife, then plunged it back in again and Derrek trembled and fell to his knees, leaning against his killer's legs.

"Where is the package?" the man hissed in heavily accented English, but Derrek didn't answer. He couldn't even if he wanted to. He couldn't even breathe.

The man pulled the knife out at last and Derrek crumpled to the floor, convulsing a bit while the man looked around the entrance of the room briefly. Derrek hadn't been any further into his room than that before he was attacked, and so the attacker realized that the package had already been delivered. He leaned back over Derrek and stared into his face. All Derrek could do was blink.

"Sleep now, my friend. Go to paradise. I am sorry I had to take your life, but it was the bidding of my Master. Be satisfied. I will probably join you soon. My Master will soon send me after you once I tell him that I have failed to retrieve the package. I hope you will not hate me in the great beyond. Maybe there at least we can be friends." The man said to Derrek and Derrek could tell what he said was true.

The man gave the room another quick look over and then left. Derrek simply laid on the floor, growing colder and more tired until, at last, he couldn't keep his eyes open anymore. He knew he was dying. He wished he had never left Prince Edward Island. He wished he had never left his barber shop. He hadn't even got to see an actual Son in the flesh and he had died for their cause.

Chapter Two
Finding Out

The Host was someone I had known for years. I had seen him at my parent's house almost daily for my entire life. He had come over to help us build our barn, I'd have to say that was my earliest memory of him, but I had many others. He had driven my brother and me to school many times when the family's car was broke down, had loaned my family money more than once when times were tough without ever wanting it back, and had delighted me more than once with scary stories and dirty jokes while my Mom would grimace at having me hear such things at such a young age. I had no reason to doubt or distrust this man whatsoever. So when Dad, Mom, and he came to me one day just after I graduated high school and told me that he was a werewolf and that my family came from a line of people that served them, I really didn't know what to think. One thing was for sure, though. I could tell that they weren't kidding.

"You have been chosen to know, and if you wish, to serve and know more," Mom said after she and Dad had told me the news. I was still skeptical, highly so, but I could tell that they themselves believed it.

"So... what would I have to do?" I asked them. I figured it was a valid question. Apparently, he did, too, judging from the look on his face. Mom and Dad looked at him, relieved that they didn't have to answer this one.

"A bit of everything, really. You might never get asked to do anything, or you might be called upon to go and remove some tracks or maybe even to go to the police department and destroy evidence, or possibly even to go and kill somebody. Who knows? That's the name of the game kiddo. We just do as we are told... And for that, we get to know things nobody else knows and to be a part of something secret and special and ancient." He told me and I looked at him curiously. I was young then, fresh out of high school, and here I was being told possibly the greatest secret of modern-day mankind.

"So... If I say yes, do I get paid or anything?" I asked and my Dad chuckled. Mom just smiled and rolled her eyes.

"No... It's kind of a volunteer-type thing. But the more you do, the more they do kind of thing. We're kind of a balance-oriented people, kiddo. But don't worry, I'll still pay you for helping me out at my place from time to time." He told me with a laugh and I shrugged and nodded in acceptance.

"What all would it entail? I'm not sure what I could do, really. How could I be of any help to a... werewolf?"

Mom grimaced, as did Dad at the "W" word. He just looked at me and chuckled. "They don't really like being called 'werewolves.' They aren't related to wolves any more than you are.

They have a few names they go by, Dominum Pa'Nok, in their own language, it means "Night Lord," but they also go by a different name. The Sons of Lycaon. As a rule they call themselves the first one, and the Son name thing basically is what the Allies call them. But definitely not "werewolf." They are a complete species, not a mix of man and animal. I'm a Host... but that's it. I can't go bite you and make you turn into one or anything. It's a different species, not some kinda venereal disease."

"Ok, so is the whole T.V. thing is bullshit? Silver bullets and full moons mean anything special?" I asked and he nodded, but with a bit of doubt.

"Silver is nasty. It's rumored to be a soul-killing substance. Every species has one, and silver is *said* to be ours. To take a soul is more than just to kill the creature it owns, it's to kill a part of God, because we feel that God is within everything. As for the full moon stuff, that maybe true for the lower breeds of my kind since they were more active during full moons, but that was because they had weaker night vision and couldn't see much at night otherwise. But there aren't many of those around anymore, thank goodness. We managed to pretty much eliminate the lower bloods over the years with the help of selective breeding, and a few other grislier methods, and now things are much safer and cleaner for everyone involved.

The lower bloods were a real threat. They would be the stereotypical mindless beasts you would call the "W" word. We still get the odd one from time to time though."

Dad spoke up then. "Ok Jackette, I don't think there is much more he can tell you at this point that you would need to know if you're not interested. Are you in, or are you out? One thing though, is that this is a life-long commitment. You can never ever really leave. You might get involved and stay in for a few years, then think you outgrew it, or you might get pissed off at them for something, or whatever, and you might decide to leave, but you don't ever really leave. You will always be monitored, spied on, and tested to see if you're keeping the secret. I've seen what happens to Allies that quit and have loose lips. They disappear. Souls get taken, family members drop off the face of the Earth, you name it. They can, and will, end your entire existence in the blink of an eye. You can leave anytime you want, provided that you keep their secrets. But if you decide to stay in the Alliance, then you will get closer and closer to them and learn more about life and existence than you ever thought possible."

Mom looked at me then and held my hand. "Honey, first thing I'll tell you is that it's not an easy road, but it is worth it, in my opinion. It's like they say; "Nothing worth hunting is ever found with ease."

I looked at him, then Mom, then Dad, then back to him again before nodding. "Ok, I'm in. What do I do?"

"We'll bring him out so you can be introduced formally, then we'll let you and him talk for a bit. You'll like him." Dad said, smiling.

"Bring who out? What do you mean?" I asked, feeling very confused all of a sudden. I half expected Mom to open the closet door and have a were... er... *Son of Lycaon* walk out into the room and shake my hand.

"Rob can channel him. He sits down and can bring Lord DeRom's consciousness forward enough so that we can talk to him. All those nights we were over at his place playing cards? That was what we were really up to. Speaking to Lord DeRom." Mom said as she motioned towards Rob who apparently was referred to as "The Imperial Host."

"Lord Who?" I asked. I hadn't heard his name said before. I never thought of them really having family names and titles and the like.

"DeRom. The ruling family. He is the current leader of his race," Rob told me. "The DeRom tends to be white-furred and yellow-eyed, although he has a black stripe down his right side from shoulder to thigh and another one from around his mid-chest running around under his right arm to the middle of his back. But you won't likely ever see him... maybe once or twice in your life possibly, but I doubt much more than that unless you get involved really heavily in the Alliance. Lower generations of Allies like you guys do not have the mental walls strong enough to protect your thoughts. Information is kept from them lower generation Allies for a reason, and sometimes false information is fed to them to confuse astral spies."

"The Alliance? You keep saying that, what is it?" I asked again, hating myself for having so many questions.

"The people who serve. Usually, people with the blood themselves, but not always. There are two branches of the Alliance really, the Grands and the Royals. We're Royals. We serve Lord DeRom exclusively. The Grand Alliance deals with all the day to day stuff the other Sons are involved with. Royals do a lot less usually." Mom told me.

"So we can actually sit down and talk to him? Is it safe? He won't try to eat us or anything, will he?" I asked and they looked a bit embarrassed by my sudden doubt and fear.

Rob just laughed and shook his head in the negative. "No Jackette, he won't eat you, highly unlikely anyway… unless you're covered in mustard or horseradish. He absolutely *loves* that stuff. And as for it being safe, well, he hasn't harmed anyone yet and he's been speaking to your folks for years now. He might ask a few inappropriate questions though, he tends to do that a bit... just answer whatever he asks of you and feel free to ask him whatever questions you have. But just remember now, he isn't me. He's just a roommate in the same house sorta thing. And he doesn't come from the same culture as you do, so be warned, he might ask or do some strange stuff. We'll be with you, so just follow our lead... well, your parent's lead. He probably won't get up and walk around or anything, and he won't change form. He's been waiting to talk to you for your whole life. He even held you once when you were a baby."

I blinked in shock a few times and then laughed. "Ok then!" I said with a gasp and Mom laughed at me and nodded. "He even gave you a nickname, "Ka'Dooog."

"What? What does it mean? Ka what?"

"Ka'Dooog." He said to me, "It means "Little Seed." I guess because you were so tiny or something."

I grinned at the nickname. I never really had one before and I kinda liked the thought that Lord DeRom had given me one before I was old enough to even walk.

I was instructed on the etiquette of speaking to a Son through its Host. Never offer food or drink to it, never ask how it is feeling, never speak to it while menstruating, never apologize unless it is one hundred percent sincere, keep your head lower than his, don't pass gas, be exceptionally polite and honest, and remember that you are talking to a being that could not only rip you limb from limb physically, but could somehow tear out your very soul and stop it from progressing as well.

It scared me, the whole soul-killing thing. Destruction of the entire spirit associated with you. No Heaven or Hell, if such places even existed, no reincarnation, no white light at the end of the tunnel, just a sudden and abrupt stop to YOU as a whole for all eternity. It terrified me then and it terrifies me just as much now, especially once you realize how much of it goes on all around us every day, and just how precious and delicate your soul truly is.

Speaking to Lord DeRom that first night was strange. It was still the same man I had grown up around just sitting there, but it wasn't him at the same time. You could tell it wasn't. The voice was different, his breathing was different, the whole feel he put off was different, and the way he carried himself was different. Everything was the same, but everything was different, all in one.

He sat cross-legged on the edge of the bed, draped in a large purple silk sheet, while Mom, Dad, and I sat on the floor in front of him. I was tempted several times to just get up and laugh and say "Bullshit!" but I didn't... and the more I sat there and listened to him speak to us, the more I believed it.

He spoke eloquently in a way, but carefully, as a person

somewhat adept in English but not like a native speaker of it would be like. He used some words that were not English, almost Latin sounding in a way, but the others seemed to know what they meant and could translate for me if needed. He used his hands strangely, the pinky finger curling across the others towards the thumb, and he hunched low and frowned a lot as he spoke at first, then loosened up as time went on and our talk rolled over the hour mark.

The most memorable thing I'd have to say, though, was his breathing and his voice, low and melodious in a sense, with deep, low breaths that seemed to be pulling air into him right down to his toes. The other memorable thing about him was that he had a deep sad feel about him, but yet he wasn't without humor.

Everyone there had nicknames in Son, with mine being "Little Seed," Dad's being "Guuu'Chaa Looo-mee" or "Water Child," and Mom's being "Pelli E'prin" fur dark, or "Dark Fur" as she was raven haired. I liked mine, and Mom liked hers, but Dad always winced slightly when he called him it and Mom would snicker. I was to find out later it was because Lord DeRom had saved Dad's life once years ago when Dad had fallen through the ice and nearly drowned, and was now always teasing him about it.

I found out that they could do strange things. The elements could tell them things, they could see things we could not, other dimensions or other realities or something like that. They could supposedly use mystical portals to travel to different places and these portals were apparently all around us. They could hear for miles, see for miles, and smell for miles. They could talk to the trees and the animals, and they could read your mind with a touch or a look. I was terrified and amazed all in one, but I still doubted the whole thing somewhat.

He wouldn't tell me much back then, just giving me bits and pieces to mull over at a time. Looking back, I suppose it was a matter of trust more than anything, that and seeing if my mental abilities could truly comprehend the whole thing. I wasn't sure, but I thought they might have bugged my phone back then to see if I was telling my friends what was going on or not, but I realized that they wouldn't need to do that if they wanted to find out things, all they would need to do would be to ask the air or something.

****

The months passed and every Wednesday we would all gather at his house to talk. Rob would bring Lord DeRom forward and we would sit down and discuss a wide variety of things. I found him to be a very good confidant, and he always gave me good advice, albeit a bit strange at times. I learned that I needed to take things with a grain of salt much of the time, especially at first, but eventually, he began telling me the whole truth about things, once I had earned his complete trust and he knew I wasn't just a 'fashionable Ally.'

That tended to happen a bit, he had told us. A 'fashionable Ally' is someone who was all gung-ho at first, but then loses interest as time goes on and they are given a few uncomfortable duties or things to do. But I had earned the respect he gave me, and he had earned mine, and I was rewarded with as much truth as I was willing to give to him in return.

"I have lived a life of both envy and unspeakable horror." He told me one night as I sat before him, writing down what he said word for word. "I have heard the subtle siren songs sung by secret races hidden in the very depths of the Earth itself, and I have heard the dying moans and screams of agony from those I held dear. Yes, Ka'Dooog, I have lived a life of envy and of horror, but I am a Dominum Pa'Nok, a "Night Lord," and a DeRom, and such is our fate.

"Werewolves, you humans call us. Mythological, Shape-shifters, Monsters, Demons, and even on rare occasions, Angels as well. We have been here as long as Man has been here, a brother race, one and the same, living with you but hidden from you at the same time. We live all over the Earth, in cities and small towns, villages and suburbs. We are your everyday citizens by day.

Policemen and cab drivers, steel workers and fishermen, farmers and merchants, and even the odd politically motivated individual as well. We are both the rich and the poor, and even the dwindling middle class, too. We are from everywhere and nowhere at the same time."

He paused then, not an uncommon thing for him. I had seen many such lapses of silence during our talks over the years and have grown used to them. It seemed to be a Son trait I was told. I had never met another Son at that point, nor even seen him in his own form. From what I heard about how they acted towards all but the mightiest and wisest Allies in the flesh, I was glad. They were an unforgiving people when it came to bending etiquette, to say the least.

He began after a bit and I resumed my writing. "Historically, I suppose we are African in a sense. Our Father's race hailed from Madagascar, although they were not indigenous to that region. I will not talk much of them, for to discuss the O'Sian's with those who are not deeply allied to our kind is forbidden. Needless to say, they are powerful, mighty, and wise. And rather arrogant at times... if the truth be told. Thankfully, they do not meddle much in our affairs."

I shivered then at hearing those words. Were there other races out there more powerful than them? A parent race? I knew the word "O'Sia" meant "Judge" in their language, and I had heard snippets of dealing with advanced technology "Not of our own making" over the years. I had a feeling I would learn much writing down the words he was saying tonight.

"There are twelve main Halls, or families, of the Sons of Lycaon and many other minor Son families that belong to them. Many of them can be identified by look once you get accustomed to seeing us in our true form. If you ever have cause to meet any of the others, I will be sure to inform you of their family line and what to look for. I will tell you a bit now though."

He paused again, letting me catch up with my scribbling. This stuff was golden if I was to be someday allowed to get more involved. I had sat at his feet every week for two years now, listening intently to the stories he told me, committing as much of it to memory as possible. He was grooming me for a higher position, Mom and Dad had told me. I was given many minor tasks since I had first joined, all usually for my own good, as well as to test my limits and loyalty.

Since I was only a fourth-generation Ally, I needed to be on special diets for months on end to help build tolerance for keeping their secrets. What a diet had to do with my ability to keep my mouth closed, I had no idea, but they also told me that they wanted me to eat special foods to help build my mind's and my body's immunity to poisons and whatnot. I was denied to watch various social media influences since they served only to weaken my minds ability to defend itself from outside spies, made to do regular physical and mental exercises, and to abstain from recreational drugs, vaping, and smoking. My duties then were simple and were likely always going to be so: Getting me to write out and deliver information for him, usually by just leaving a letter in a jar someplace to be picked up by another Ally later on.

But I had no other actual contact with the Alliance other than with my parents, and with the Host. I hadn't even seen a Son in the flesh and remembered it. Apparently, they could "Charm" a person into not remembering that they were seen. Even get the person to tell them things or go places and do tasks without remembering them. I knew it wasn't bullshit, though. I remember one time going to bed out in my tent one night to deliver a note, then waking up in my house and the note being gone. When I had asked about it I was simply told that Lord DeRom had decided to deliver it himself and that I had assisted him. I wanted nothing more than to see a Son in the flesh or even to talk to another Ally, but I was always told that I was lucky not to be involved more than I was. My family wasn't a high enough generation yet.

He inhaled and looked down at me and I prepared to write again. I did what I could to keep up. Luckily, I had been smart enough to start learning shorthand years ago and I was glad I did. He told me all about the sacred rules that they all try to observe and the holy times they follow, and then he started telling me a bit about the other noble families. I wrote and wrote until he finally decided enough was enough, then he stopped for another long pause. My arm was sore from writing now. I wished he would allow us to record him, but when I asked about it, he simply shook his head and said that previous Allies had tried it and it proved to be a bad idea.

He inhaled deeply and I could tell that he was readying himself to speak.

"My family is the white-furred ruling family that keeps the rest focused on our common enemies and goals instead of fighting amongst ourselves. There are two branches of the family, noble and common, but we are all one Hall. We are called the "Solvers of Puzzles" by the other families. We are the mystics and rulers of the Sons of Lycaon, and while we are loved by our people, we are forever kept apart from them. Ours is a sad, lonely life. Filled with terror and sorrow and beauty, all intermixed together as one. It is said that the DeRom all die alone, and in all the years my family has been, we have never seen it to be false."

He grew quiet then and I didn't press him for more information. We sat in silence for several uncomfortable minutes and he finally began to speak again.

"Only the DeRom may rule, for only they have the minds for it." He said after a pause and then grew quiet again. He seemed lost in thought. He often did.

He stopped then and left after a bit of simple chatter once he made sure everything had been written down. I was glad, because I had severe writer's cramp now and my arm was killing me. Our talk had been over three hours long this time, and I looked up at Rob, who awoke looking groggy and slightly confused... and sleepy.

I asked him once what he does when he goes into the trance before Lord DeRom comes out, and he told me that as soon as he drops into the trance, he sees fog and in the fog, a rock about 4 feet high. He goes to the rock and sits there and it is there that Lord DeRom comes to him. Sometimes gently, sometimes ferociously, but always he comes, and as soon as they touch, Lord DeRom takes control of the body and Rob is left in the fog on the rock until he returns. The rock apparently serves as an anchor between the physical and astral realms.

I asked him once if he could hear or see us while he's in there and he said that usually no, but that sometimes Lord DeRom would allow him to hear and see what is going on. He then said that he didn't like that, though, because it is very unsettling to see and hear second-hand from your own body.

Actually, I was glad he couldn't hear us because sometimes I would tell Lord DeRom some incredibly personal things. He was good for that kind of thing, actually. I could tell him my feelings about this and that or things I had done and he would never condemn me or anything, only tell me how things could be better if I had done certain things differently or give me a unique insight into how the other person could react or feel. He had become my best friend in a way.

I looked up at Rob and smiled at him and he grinned and then stretched and winced as he always did after Lord DeRom and I had one of our longer chats. Lord DeRom could sit for hours and hours cross-legged as he spoke, I don't know how, but poor Rob always suffered immediately afterwards as he untied his legs from the position and groaned.

"So... what all did you guys talk about tonight?" he asked after a bit and I shrugged. "Just told me a bunch of stuff about the various families and the laws they follow. Kind of weird to think about them being scientists and thinkers and stuff, but I suppose it's logical. "

"Oh yeah, they are actually really contemplative in their own way. They aren't just a bunch of crazy bastards running around in the woods. Incredibly smart. We tested Lord DeRom once with an I.Q. test, just out of curiosity. One fifty-six... And he fumbled around quite a bit with language and understanding what we were asking him. He's not even really a super smart one, either. The DeRom are smart, don't get me wrong, just that they are more diplomatic than anything else. The Sons have been around a long time... They developed a culture, they have science and tech that would boggle our minds in ways, excellent medics when it comes to herbs, and they have some pretty neat-looking art. Religion and Philosophy, too. Way advanced when you think about it."

"Ok, so, he mentioned vampires before... Are they talking about real honest-to-goodness blood-drinking vampires here?" I asked him nervously and he just nodded.

"Oh yeah, there are loads of vampires out there. Not exactly your classic Bram Stoker types though. They can't fly, they aren't immortal, and they aren't hundreds of years old. They also don't blow up in daylight, a lot of them are hard-core churchgoers, and they can eat garlic. Heck, I even dated one for a while when I was around your age. Sweet gal. Hot as hell... but it was frowned upon... heavily. We had to call it quits. Fun while it lasted, though. Damn fun. Poor girl is dead now. Shame."

"So, how many are we talking here? Hundreds?" I asked him, feeling a tad nervous about going home in the dark all of a sudden.

"Oh hell no, tens of thousands more likely. Never did get an exact number of them, more than likely never will. Every so often, they get brazen and try to pull some stunt on us to get more rights or blackmail us and we need to go and cull out a bunch of them." He said nonchalantly. It unnerved me that he could talk about murder so carelessly, but Host's tended to be a bit hardened towards that type of thing. They had a duty to exterminate the evil and corrupt, so they spent a lot of their time bathed in blood, according to him. I thought it made them a bit too cavalier towards death.

"How many Sons are there?" I asked him. I figured with tens of thousands of vampires out there, there had to be that many or more of them. It wasn't normally like me to ask such direct questions regarding abilities and numbers... I was always told this was sort of a secret area. Understandably.

He didn't seem to mind, though. He trusted me. "Oh... let's see... Son's... about two or three hundred worldwide, at best guess... maybe two-three thousand Alpha's... but that's anybody's guess. A lot of those guys live WAY out in the bush."

"Just two or three hundred? That's it? How do you manage to control the vampires when they cause trouble?" I was confused. It just didn't seem to fit.

"Because TV is full of shit." He said with a chuckle. "We're a lot more powerful than they are, and they are a lot weaker than they are portrayed in books and movies. Hell, a good Alpha should be able to take out six or seven vampires in hand-to-hand combat alone, not to mention the mental abilities we have that they don't."

I knew what an Alpha was, the offspring of two Son parents.

Able to shapeshift with ease, do partial shifts, and even do practically instantaneous shifts. They were strictly bipedal, like a person, unlike the more gorilla-like Son body form. They also were much weaker mentally and slower physically. They didn't have dual minds. However, Alphas were one being, and not two separate entities like a true Son was. It made for a totally different creature but the same in culture, language and society. Each had their own unique strengths and weaknesses.

"Vampires are not like those eighteenth-century fancy, frilly lace-wearing types you see on T.V., my dear. They don't turn into animals or bats or mist or any of that jazz. Really, the only real thing that they have over a human is about double the strength and endurance. Night vision is better of course, and hearing as well, but that's about it. But a well-trained human can sometimes kick the crap out of the average vampire. The average Son is what, four or five times stronger than a vamp? And with our mental abilities, way more deadly. It would be no sweat to wipe out a dozen or more in combat and one of our highly skilled guys, twenty or higher, and that'd be without using weapons." He said to me, and I thought about it for a minute then piped up.

"So what all can vampires do?"

He leaned back and then pulled on a T-shirt and his socks and pants before he told me. "A Vamp can make you forget you've seen him sometimes, like how we charm, and they can blend in way better to human society than we can, obviously. They say that they can see through the eyes of their masters, something they call "spelling," but we figure that's about it for their mind tricks. They have a few other little tricks that don't work on us and only work about half the time on humans, but not much more. They might have more in another few thousand years if they decided to do some selective breeding, but they sure aren't practicing any restraint in that area."

I let this absorb before I asked my next question, still depending on what I had seen on T.V. "But aren't they rich and stuff? All the vampires on T.V. live in castles and stuff."

"Most of them are dirt poor. I'd say ninety-nine percent of them. They are literally owned by their higher families, who use them as slave labor. The high-end vamps live high on the hog with it and almost nothing goes back to help their people. Do you think you have it rough? Son females and our female Allies are given total equality. Sure, Son females are not allowed into higher-level government areas, but the males aren't allowed into the higher-level church areas. It's a balance of power thing and it's all half and half. Vampires on the other hand, consider themselves a male-only race. Vampire females are simply used as trading items and for sex. And to boot, they practice incest like it's an art form. Thankfully for the females they can control their menstrual cycle... they can't get pregnant unless they want to. Their human female Allies? They are usually short lived unless they have the skills they need. Otherwise, they are usually repeatedly raped and fed upon until they die. Period."

"That's horrible! How do they even attract Allies?" I asked him with horror. He just laughed somewhat angrily.

"Well, they have good old T.V. working for them, remember? Before you came into the Alliance, if we would have asked you what race was stronger or cooler, vampire or werewolf, you probably would have said vampire. They have been heavily romanticised over the years. They are seen as sensual and powerful. You wanna know something funny? Do you want to know what the number one cause of death is for new vampires who changed without having an elder around to show them the ropes? Falling. You wanna know why? They were jumping off of buildings and shit thinking they could fly. I actually sent one of the more popular vampire novel writers a "thank you" postcard. Never said why or gave my name or anything, just a little postcard with thank you written on it and a picture of wolves on the other side."

I was laughing hard by this point, picturing some newly changed vampire leaping off of the roof of their apartment building and then smashing head-first into the ground. This led me to my next question. "So... what happens to all these dead vampires? Don't people find them and say, "Holy shit, this guy isn't human!" I know I would be kinda freaked out... and I know about them."

"Well, I'd be lying if I said none of them ever get discovered or seen and stuff, but that's what Allies are for... Cleaning up our messes. And our mitochondria tend to revert us back to our human forms upon our deaths... Sometimes..." he said as he folded up the purple robe and put the lights back on. Talking to Lord DeRom was always done in dim light.

"Mito... who? Are they some other Allied group? Some type of ambulance workers or something?" I asked him and he burst out laughing.

"Skip biology class much? No, no, hell no... mitochondria... They're the things that power the cells in everybody. Everyone has them, not just us. They kinda make electricity. Didn't you take biology in school? We get the energy needed to shapeshift from ours. I guess that means we are electrically powered or something. It could be interesting to see one of us get the electric chair..."

I felt stupid then but laughed along with him. He had so much wisdom inside of him, he just knew SO MUCH about this stuff that I felt dumb being around him. But he never made me feel stupid, though. He teased me about some things, but always in a good-natured way.

We got dressed in our outdoor clothes and walked out to his

old truck so he could drive me home. It was a cool autumn night, early October, and the leaves were starting to fly off of the trees and decorate everyone's lawns. People were putting out their Halloween decorations and farmers were kicking their gears in overdrive to get the last of their potato crops in. He paused at the side of his truck and looked up at the star filled sky. I looked up as well.

"Makes you feel small, doesn't it," I said to him after a few seconds of silent star gazing. He shook his head in the negative.

"Nope, not really. Flattered. Glad that God thought to make me amidst all that other stuff going on out there. One of our ancient ones said that those who can look up at the stars and not feel humbled are either the master of all of them or the biggest fool under them. I always liked that saying. Keeps you aware of God, I figure... let's you know that you weren't just made by accident... that everything has a purpose for being and that it's up to you to realize that. You can accept the fact that God made you in some sort of plan, or you can just look up at the stars and think nothing and be on your merry, ignorant way. I prefer to look up and say, 'thanks for making me. I'll try my best to do what I can to make this a better place.'"

I got in the truck then and Rob drove me home. I didn't live far, really, not quite a mile down the road, but it was dark, and he knew I didn't like walking alone, especially at night. Being a Son Ally tends to make you a tad nervous at night... especially once you've heard how some of the families like to hunt down and kill people just for being out at night and whatnot. Apparently there was an ancient treaty made between Son's and Man to avoid each other's times. Man needed the day so they could hunt and raise crops and so the Sons made a deal to only go out an hour after sunset and to be in an hour before the sun rose, or so the story went. Some of the stricter families were said to like enforcing that treaty at every opportunity, and our area was possibly due for a Son visitation since Lord DeRom had recently allowed visiting Sons to visit his region.

Rob dropped me off at the door of my house, then pointed at our dog. "Better let Laddie sleep in the house. There's supposed to be a group of Sons coming to the grounds tonight." He told me and then waved goodbye to me once he seen that I had opened the door and made it in safely.

I still lived with my parents even though I had graduated from school and was old enough to be on my own, but I stayed mostly because I had to help them with their farm since my brother had got hit by a car and died when he was fourteen. Dad and Mom were both in their mid-forties now, and since I wasn't really the student type anyway, I volunteered to stay home to help them out. It wasn't like they were old or anything, forty is hardly old, but the farm kept us all pretty busy, so it would have only been worse without me.

I went to the fridge and poured myself a glass of milk and then went to the washroom and got ready for bed. I made sure Laddie, our golden retriever, was in for the night as well, scared to leave her out anymore since I heard that Sons liked the taste of dog lung. I knew Lord DeRom wouldn't have done anything to him, but with the extra Sons in our area, I didn't want to take the chance.

I laid in my bed and let my mind wander. A part of me doubted him... doubted he even existed. I hadn't seen anything, or even met another Ally other than my parents. Could he be faking the whole thing? I was running on hearsay completely. What had I actually seen with my own two eyes? Nothing. I'd never seen another Ally, a vampire, an Alpha, or a Son. I hadn't seen ANYTHING supernatural. I'd just spent hundreds of hours of my time sitting on the floor like an idiot, listening to some guy talk to me in a strange voice, claiming to be king of the werewolves. He could have been making it all up, he'd have one helluva imagination if he did, but it *was* possible.

A part of me felt bad for thinking this way... but what if it was true? Had he been scamming Mom and Dad, too? For how long had he been playing this little game? Sure, I had experienced some weird stuff, like waking up in a different place that one time, but I could have been drugged.

"Drugged!" I gasped to myself. Sure, I could have been

drugged! He could have given me something in a drink or something and just waited till I passed out and carried me home! I wasn't a fat girl by any stretch of the imagination, I was barely over a hundred pounds and Rob was, what... double my size? Sure, he could have picked me up and taken me home! But... what if he did other stuff to me, too? God, could he have raped me too? Raped me while I was unconscious? I was still a virgin... at least, I thought I was. You couldn't lose your virginity and not feel it the next day, could you?

I had been in this "Alliance" of his for just about two years now. Mom and Dad had been in it for much longer. I kicked myself for having possibly wasted the last two years of my life playing disciple to some crazy loner who thought he was the king of the werewolves.

But what if he wasn't lying? I often had suspicions that it was all some twisted joke gone wrong. I often doubted, but it always seemed so real… I had to find out the truth, and settle these thoughts of mine once and for all. I was losing my mind. I had found myself going through moments like this more and more lately. Doubts and fears were driving me over the deep end. But as long as I went through my life without actually seeing one, any of them, I would wonder if he had lied to us.

I slipped from my bed and got dressed in a pair of dark jeans and a pair of my old hiking boots. I put on a plain black turtleneck and then got a hat and pair of gloves from the closet and an old denim coat and then slipped downstairs once again.

I had a vague idea of where I would go if I wanted to see some proof. I also knew that if they were, in fact real, I could be charmed and not remember any of this. But I also knew how to negate the effects of charming. Be drunk.

I opened up the liquor cabinet and stole a pint of gin from its teakwood depths. I took three large drinks of it, gagging the entire time, but managed to keep it down. I took the remaining half of it with me, tucked away in my backpack, where I also tossed in a flashlight and a bottle of "no-scent" that Dad used for hunting deer over across the mainland.

The deer are extinct where we live. We live in rural Prince Edward Island, up at the western end, and there was no real wildlife left. No bears, no elk, no moose, and no deer. All we had for wildlife other than birds were skunks, raccoons, coyotes, and foxes, basically. There were no worries of attack by anything other than other people and of course, these mythological creatures, if they indeed existed at all.

I covered myself with the "no-scent" and headed down the long lonely road towards the Host's house. I didn't use the flashlight, or make any unnecessary noises. Every so often, I would take another nip out of the gin bottle to keep the slight edge going that I had and before long, I was once again at his home.

His woods were beautiful in the daytime. Park-like. They were located across a small field and was just in the back of his house, an area that he said was Lord DeRom's private grounds. I had been there dozens of times in the day time and it was actually quite relaxing, well-groomed and painstakingly cared for. No dead trees lying down, all the ground was clear of debris, with very nice trails throughout the whole wooded territory.

I found a nice quiet area out by the edge of the woods, with me being just barely inside the tree line, lying down beside a small thicket of ground hemlock. From my vantage point I could see the area between the small personal grounds and the larger forest a few dozen acres away. Between the two was a large field full of wild grass and clover, mostly just pasture for livestock, and I could pretty much see right across that field to the big forest with no major difficulty, if whatever I was looking at was taller than the grass.

From my hiding spot, I could also see his house perfectly. He had an old, two-story farmhouse with a few old sheds out back. A light was on in the bedroom upstairs where we usually did our talks, and I wondered what he was doing up there. He lived alone except for his dog "Moon" and a few barn cats that stayed outside and were half-wild. I didn't know for certain if he had family in the area, but I didn't think so. I did know for a fact that he did have siblings, but most of them lived off the island. He claimed he was the only one of his siblings to carry the Son gene however, so little else was mentioned of his human family. Terribly convenient if he was full of shit.

At about three-thirty, I woke up from a light doze. I was disoriented and not sure where I was for a second, and I cursed myself for having fallen asleep. I looked at the house and noticed the bedroom light was off now. How long it had been off, I had no idea, but I had been out for almost two hours now. I shifted in position a bit to alleviate the cramp I was getting in my legs and then froze in place.

Something was moving in the field! Something large! It wasn't cow large, though, which was my first thought, but it was definitely as large as a fairly big person. I took another huge gulp of the gin, killing the bottle, and fought to gasp in the air quietly as I stared at the shape, moving slowly through the field. I calmed myself down as much as I could, but a huge part of me was kicking my ass for doubting. If they sensed me, they'd likely kill me instantly... if I was lucky.

The shape moved slowly, carefully walking through the field, somewhat low to the ground. I fought to see better, but it was dark and the shape was low in the grass, barely over the tops. I could see a head sort of, and I thought I might have seen the shape of a snout, but I couldn't be sure. And I had to be sure. After all, it could theoretically be a dog or something, albeit a really large dog like a Great Dane or a bent-over man walking through the field with a mask on or something. I was grasping at straws at that point, I know, but unless I had an absolute 100% view, I would always have doubts.

I waited a few more seconds before I noticed another shape coming from the same direction I had seen the first one come from. The first one was still now, just standing in the field, waiting for the second one to catch up. The second one moved slowly like the first one had done, walking painstakingly slowly through the field until it had joined the first one. It was then that I noticed three more of them coming through the field towards the other two, this time all moving much, much faster and running low.

They quickly rejoined with the first two and the five of them moved stealthily towards the house. Since the house was closer to me than it was to them, they slowly came closer and closer into view. By the time they were at the house, I no longer had any doubts.

I watched the five Sons approach his lawn and then stop. One of them left the group in the long grass and made its way onto the short grass of his lawn and that was when I could get a decent view of its form.

The being was about five and a half feet tall, but it was

obviously hunched over. If it were totally upright, I would not doubt that it would have been about another foot taller. I couldn't really estimate weight, but it was large, and it had a tight stomach and an exceptionally thick chest and an extremely thick back hump, the way Lord DeRom, Rob, and my parents had all described.

There was a snout, sloping down more from the high forehead area, not jutting straight out from the face like a dog's snout does. I could kind of make out ears, pointed up and out slightly, and the legs were just strange. At one moment, when they first came out of the long grass, they were short, but when they got out of the grass and onto the lawn, it seemed as if they grew and straightened or something, then I realized that they went from running on fours to walking on two legs. There seemed to be no heel of the foot whatsoever and an incredibly large powerful set of thighs and calves. They ran much the same way a gorilla would.

The shock was just starting to wear off when the one on the lawn suddenly reached up in the air and then moved its hand down like it was pulling down a zipper, and a large rip appeared out of nothing. The Son entered it then and disappeared.

The other Sons approached the hole in nothing and one by one, they all walked into it and vanished along with the hole itself. When the last one was gone, I waited for another half hour, then looked around carefully for any more movement. Seeing none, I made my way slowly back to the road and then ran home.

I vaguely remember the walk home. I half walked, half ran the entire way, terrified and ecstatic and half drunk at the same time. It *hadn't* been bullshit. I WAS a part of something incredible, and my parents and Rob hadn't been filling me full of shit all this time. I got home and half-tripped, going up the stairs to my room, cursing myself for making so much noise and praying I didn't wake up Mom and Dad. When I was certain that I had awoken no one, I resumed my voyage up the stairs to my room and shut the door behind me, still shaking with excitement.

Chapter Three
The Emerald Isle

It was late the next morning when I awoke, not having slept after I got home last night from all the excitement. I woke to the sound of Mom driving the tractor out to the field to feed the cows. I made my way downstairs and found breakfast cooked and in the fridge for me. I ate without reheating it and then immediately went to Rob's house.

He answered the pounding door somewhat angrily and I could tell at once that I had just woke him up. Soon as he seen me, his anger left. "Jackette... what's wrong? Come on in." He said to me, noting my excitement.

"I just wanted to say I'm sorry for doubting you. I used to think that maybe you were making it all up for some reason, so last night, I went to your grounds and waited and seen five of them enter a portal right in your backyard! You weren't... I mean... Lord DeRom wasn't one of those guys, was he?"

He looked at me, sort of confused, still half asleep, then shook his head. "No... I never shifted last night. Did they have black fur? That was probably some of the Wara clan. They said they would be around the grounds. How did you not get seen? Or Charmed? You're crazy! If that was the V'Lin family, you would be dead right now! They *hate* humans! Hell, if those Wara would have seen you, *they* probably would have killed you!"

"I drank some gin and used Dad's "no-scent" that he uses for hunting. I hid over in the bushes by your grounds. I hope you're not mad at me! I just HAD to see for myself! I'm really sorry, I am... I just had to know a hundred percent." I said to him, feeling pretty stupid and low. He was right. If I was spotted by those guys last night, they would have killed me. Royal Ally or not. There were ways to do things and that was most definitely NOT the right way to go about things. But it HAD worked, and I no longer had any doubts... and I think he was kinda impressed that I had pulled it off.

He shook his head in disbelief and then just surrendered and laughed. "Gin and no-scent... good Lord... wait until I tell them they were spotted by a novice Ally using gin and no-scent... they'll never hear the end of it!"

He looked at me then and lost the smile. "So... now that you have no more doubts... what are your next plans? These things usually escalate. Touch one? Join up with one of the religious Sept's and join a cause. Go hunting vampires? Go out on a midnight meeting?"

I didn't know how to react. Was he serious? I'd LOVE to go to a meeting! I had heard Mom and Dad talk about when they had seen Lord DeRom in person... they had to have a drink of some noxious stuff... to keep from being charmed... and then, they were led by a High Ally to meet with him. They were only allowed to be so close, maybe fifty or sixty feet away, no metals were allowed, and all questions had to be relayed through the High Ally. Apparently, it was the way the first meetings were done for centuries between Son's and Humans. I would have LOVED to have seen that!

"Well, considering your resourcefulness, I could arrange some sort of meeting to take place. Your Son is fluent now, you speak it pretty much as well as any human can. Lord DeRom will be meeting with a vampire unit in a few weeks. I'll ask him about you possibly joining in and taking part as his aide. His English is a bit rough to say the least and I doubt they speak Son any more than he speaks vamp." he said to me and I screamed in delight and bounced around the room like a maniac. I had been learning the Son language since day one pretty much and I was almost fluent in it. I just wasn't sure how it would sound coming from the mouth of Lord DeRom himself, not Rob's.

The weeks passed and I was slowly initiated into being an Aide. I learned how Lord DeRom wanted everything done. Rob, Mom, Dad and I re-enacted every possible scenario of how the meeting would be. I was to stand slightly in front of and to the left of him at all times. I was never to make eye contact with the vampires while they were speaking to him, and I was to expect to be called everything under the book because I was a female. I didn't expect this to be an issue unless things went bad, and neither did the others. The vampire chauvinism was more likely than not going to be overruled by their utter terror of Son's... especially of Lord DeRom himself.

I was told not to second guess his words. What he said was absolute and was expected to be followed completely and utterly without any whining, refusals, or delay. He was a king after all, and kings were to be obeyed completely. It wouldn't look good on me or him if I was disobedient or showed hesitation.

I asked Mom what exactly that all meant precisely and Mom said that it was possible, not likely, but possible, that Lord DeRom could offer one or several of the vampires to sample my blood or even to have me sexually, or both. My heart raced and a huge lump in my stomach appeared instantly, when she told me this.

"You're on the pill, right?" she asked me and I nodded. I had been on it since I was sixteen, but that wasn't the issue. The issue was that I was still a virgin. When I told Mom this, she blanched and then laughed. "Well, I'm glad to see that all my preaching has paid off! I'll make sure to tell Lord DeRom this or Rob. It might save your neck... well, not your neck maybe, but possibly the other part we were discussing."

The night came at last for the meeting to take place. I still hadn't seen Lord DeRom in person, or a Son up close, or a vampire for that matter, and here I was about to be thrust into a potentially lethal situation with only theoretical knowledge at my disposal.

Mom and Dad gave me a huge farewell dinner the night before the meeting, but the night of the meeting I was instructed not to eat much and to limit my diet to certain foods so my breath wasn't overly repulsive to Lord DeRom since he would be so close to me. We then drove over to Rob's house so I could get ready. I was bathed in special water, then rubbed down with rubbing alcohol and vinegar, and then rubbed down with special oils to make my scent as non-invasive as possible. I was then given special silk robes to wear: green, orange, and pale blue, with a purple sash around my waist.

It was downright horrific in a color sense. It was explained to me that the purple symbolized that I was associated with Royalty, the green symbolized that I was Allied, the orange symbolized that I was an Aide, and the blue symbolized I was Human. I wasn't sure who exactly this was supposed to inform, since Lord DeRom could only see in black and white with a few hues of red and green, and the vampires likely knew nothing of the finer points of Son culture. As far as they knew, the Sons just killed whomever and whatever they wished dead and then disappeared back into the mists. Little of them were known to the lower-ranked vampires from what I was told, other than a few tales told to keep the guards awake and alert.

Having robes of such un-matching and horrific colors was no use at all, really.

The front of the outfit was emblazoned with the DeRom family crest. A large "Z" shape with what looked kind of like a sword going through it from top to bottom. The hilt part of the sword curled up at either end and flanking both sides of the "Z", about mid-way down, were two diamond shapes. The symbol was all done in black, red and silver. It at least looked neat, unlike my own Aide symbol.

The Aide symbol was also on my robes, on the back. It consisted of what looked like a large black checkmark with a horizontal line going across the short end of the checkmark. It wasn't anything special looking by a long shot.

I was then given soft, moccasin-styled shoes to wear. They had somewhat of a hard sole, but they were soft enough not to make noise if walking over a hard surface. They were insanely comfortable but kind of strange-looking. They were made of what resembled deer hide, but I was told they were not. Inside was lined with a very luxurious fur, which I thought could have been rabbit fur, but I was told it was not as well. When I did ask, I was told by my father; "I'm not sure, but knowing them, it's probably wiser to not know."

I got the same response when I asked what was in the drink

they told me to take. Rob had made it and left it in a mason jar on his counter with a note telling me to drink this about half an hour before going out to wait for Lord DeRom. It was utterly disgusting in every way possible. Texture-wise it was thick and had gross, crunchy, meaty chunks in it, like I was drinking something made up of dead animals. Color-wise, it was red, blood red, with slightly orange-colored chunks in it. If I looked in it carefully, I would have seen green bits in it, as well as the odd bit of white, and a few recognizable pieces of bumble bees, but I didn't look carefully at it... I hardly looked at it at all. Taste-wise, well, that was beyond description. It was coppery metallic with a hint of mint and some sort of really heavy overpowering spice like chili powder or something. I managed to get it down and keep it down and then a warm feeling came over me and washed down my whole body like a warm pail of water being slowly dumped over me.

"Whoa! Weird!" I said to my parents, who were there with me at Rob's place. "I just got a huge wave of the tingles going all through me!"

"That's normal. You might start to feel warm, too." Dad said. "It will make you unable to be affected by charming and whatever else and help kill pain if need be," he said to me as he hugged me. It was a rare show of emotion from my father.

"I love you, Jackette. Be careful, and remember your

training!" he said to me with a cracking voice. I hugged him back, fighting back my own tears.

"I will Daddy. I love you, too. Both of you," and then reached out for Mom to hug her.

They finished dressing me in the Aide clothes Rob left for me and then they left to go home. I waited almost twenty minutes more until Rob's big grandfather clock struck one A.M., and then I left to wait in the backyard for Lord DeRom.

Rob had already gone out to the forest to shift when Mom, Dad, and I had arrived at his house. Shifting apparently was a hugely painful process, taking upwards of forty-five minutes for him to perform. It was not uncommon for Host's to endure slow and hugely painful shifts if they carried Son's. Alpha's on the other hand, took almost no time. Some few Sons could shift painlessly as well, albeit not nearly as fast as an Alpha could, but for Lord DeRom, it was a long, painful, and drawn-out process that was both dangerous to perform and potentially deadly to watch. Apparently, the control part of the brain was one of the last parts to change and for about two minutes initially after the change, Lord DeRom was totally insane.

I stood in the backyard overlooking the field and stared off at the forest for some sign of him. I was nervous, but my stomach was calm. I assumed it was the effects of the drugs kicking in. I went over the list of things to do and say and all the etiquette I knew about Sons and vampires while I waited. I assumed the vampires would show up soon and we would meet in the forest out back to discuss whatever needed to be done.

I stood out there for nearly ten minutes before noticing a figure walking through the field towards me. I watched it carefully for a few seconds, my heart beginning to race wildly. "Holy shit, Holy Shit, HOLY SHIT!" I thought as it approached and I could see it more and more clearly. It was him, no doubt at all.

I waited until he was about twenty feet away before I knelt in the proper way I had been showed. It was awkward, extremely so. Right foot on the ground, right knee bent, and the left leg as far back as possible. Both forearms pressed to the earth, and my head tilted back as far as possible, exposing my throat with my eyes closed. I was totally at his mercy in that insane position, finding it difficult to stay in it without falling over. My muscles ached and I strained to remain in it, but I was told I had to stay in it until he touched my shoulder and told me to rise, and so I did.

His hand felt strange on my shoulder. Heavy, strong, and rough, like an animal's paw pad, except he had long powerful fingers with claws, and then the voice ripped into my mind, pushing away all other thoughts. "Ka'Dooog," I heard the voice say, and I nodded, then I said yes in Son. "Rise."

I opened my eyes then and stared at the large hand on my shoulder. I could feel the sheer power in it. It was like a bear's paw and a human's hand had gotten blended together somehow. It was easily twice as thick as a man's hand, with thick black pads on the palms and bottoms of his fingers and blindingly white fur on the top. At the ends of his fingers were claws, about two to three inches long, yellowish in color, with black flecks throughout them. They weren't like fingernails though, they seemed to be more like protrusions of the bone itself coming out from his outer knuckles. They were strong like the rest of him and both beautiful and deadly like him as well.

I stood and looked at him, my heart racing. He was magnificent and yet terrifying to behold, like looking at a great white shark or something. He just exuded a feeling of raw power and total control. He looked regal, he felt regal, Hell, he even sounded regal.

"I am Lord Brav'Dos DeRom of the Dominum Pa'Nok." The voice said to me without making an actual sound. It was completely telepathic, all done through touch. I was told this was how they communicated for the most part, but verbal communication was done as well. This way was much easier, though. I just wished I could have replied the same way, but I was told it must be done verbally by me.

"Introductions!" I thought and then nodded. "I am Jackette MacNeill, daughter of Eliza and Steve MacNeill, your faithful

Allies," I said in Son. I realized then that my accent was horrific but I had the vocabulary and grammar down pat. I would try to fix it as I went along. It was kinda hard to sound right without a snout. "How do you wish me to serve?"

He waited a second or two for my words to sink in and then he replied with that overriding mental voice of his. "We go to meet with the Du'o'trada to tell them of the Council's decision. Be warned, they may not take kindly to a "ma'taa si'soba mar'ii" female as my aide."

"Ma'taa si'soba mar'ii" I thought. "Mother's babies blood," that's it. Ma'taa si'soba translated to "Mother's Babies", or "humans." The Du'o'trada were the vampires, or "two teeth," as the Sons called them. They had other, less polite words for them as well. I gathered my thoughts for a second, then replied. "This ma'taa si'soba mar'ii will do all she can to honor the DeRom in this meeting with the Du'o'trada." I replied and he grunted with his actual voice and I took it to be a good thing.

He broke contact with me and then walked to where I saw the Wara use the portal. He came to a spot and I noticed a strange-looking pattern of rocks on the ground. Once I caught up with him, he spoke to me with his actual voice. "Tis Portaz. Oon Ee'nus," he said to me, pointing at the stone pattern and I nodded. "Moon door. You come." he had told me. My heart raced wildly. This meeting wasn't going to be just out in his backwoods!

I watched him close his deep golden eyes and his brow furrowed as he concentrated for a moment. He reached up and then slid his hand down, opening up a portal in thin air just like one would open up a large zipper. I knew only a few select Sons were powerful enough to trigger the portals. Every family had a few members that could open them, of course, but not every Son could, and no Alphas were even remotely powerful enough to open them on their own.

I stood in front of this thing, amazed at it. It swirled like heat waves off of a hot stretch of highway, except so much you couldn't see the other side clearly. He walked in then and I inhaled deeply and followed.

Going through the portal was anti-climactic. I was expecting a huge rush of light or something, but it was just as if I walked through a doorway in my own house. No tingles, no lights, just a slight popping in my ears and a vague weirdness of being in his lawn one minute and in a cave the next. The air felt weird, just from the suddenness of it, and I smelled ozone strongly, but that was it. The portal stayed open until he shut it the same way he had opened it, basically, except in reverse.

The cave was dank and dark with little light. Mice scurried along the floor and I could hear them squealing off in the distance, but I tuned out my revulsion to them and followed him without a moment's hesitation.

It was more of a tunnel, I realized once my eyes adjusted better to the gloom. I could hear noises and see light off in the distance, firelight I figured from the look of it, further down the tunnel. We made our way towards it.

We walked side by side, and I noticed that he sort of hopped along somewhat oddly on two legs. I had heard and seen that they were very, very fast, on all fours. But Lord DeRom seemed to almost hobble on two legs, each step bouncing its way to the next. It wasn't like he was limping or unsteady or anything, just that it seemed like it was not usual for him to be on two legs.

I took the time then to stare at him as he walked. He was covered in a robe from neck to floor for the most part, but his forearms were pretty much bare. The robe came equipped with a hood, and it was beautiful to look at as a whole. It was made of the same silky material mine was made of, except his was a pale blue to represent that he was the official spokesman to humanity for his race. All around the cuffs and the bottom was a white trim on which were dozens of Son glyphs representing the elements and various nature spirits the DeRom family worshipped. He was severely hunchbacked, or so it seemed, but this was not a deformity. Rather, it was simply the way they were built. I had been told that they were all like that and that their large back and chests gave them incredible strength for side movements like swats. I had heard that they were capable of swatting the head right off of a person with relative ease, and after seeing him up close, I had no doubts at all about that.

His fur was blindingly white, odd, I thought for a creature that lives at night, but I doubted that he really had many worries about being seen, considering he could Charm a person into forgetting he was even there. He had super thick chest and back muscles and his legs were blocky and very powerful-looking as well. I couldn't get a good look at his feet due to the long robe, but I did see his tracks in the dirt of the tunnel floor and they seemed to be like fan shapes; well spread out toes, long and strong like his fingers, with no heel whatsoever.

Regarding his hands, it was interesting to note that he seemed to have no pinky finger, but rather, another thumb. It explained why, when we spoke to him through Rob that, his own pinky fingers would always curl over his other three fingers, because in Son form, that was what they did.

His eyes were something hard to describe. One look into his golden-colored eyes with their long horizontally slit pupil let you know that this was no animal. The only other eye I have ever seen, even remotely similar to his, was a goat's eye. It seemed as if you could see right through the eye itself to a golden-colored part in the back or something. They almost seemed to glow they were so gold colored, and the long, black pupil went horizontally across the entire eye, and it seemed to widen and narrow depending on various things such as mood or lighting.

I was told that he had a large black stripe of fur going down from his right shoulder to his right thigh and another stripe intersecting it horizontally at mid-belly to the center of his back, going around the right side as well. Since he had the robe on, though, I could not see it at the time.

We made our way at last to the end of the tunnel and my eyes widened in a strange blend of horror, amusement, and disgust at what I seen. There were several male vampires in the large cave, at least a dozen, and several girl vampires in there as well that appeared to be in their late teens, to early twenties. Some were engaging in blatant sexual acts right in front of the others and us, while others still lounged around on large rugs with pillows like you would expect in harems. Damaged plastic lawn chairs and old car seats were scattered around the cave for seating, as well as for beds.

An eighties-style ghetto blaster hung off of a wire suspended from some unseen spot higher up one of the cave walls, but it was playing no music that I'd ever heard before. It sounded like some sort of screeching violin, poorly played bagpipes, and a very loud, very fast bass guitar. Every so often, the singer would screech some odd words in what I assumed was their language four or five times, and the tune would start all over again. It was far from melodic.

We stood there for a few moments watching the scene until someone noticed us and shut the ghetto blaster off. An older-looking male vampire stepped forward, pushing away a girl younger than me who had just finished giving him fellatio. He tucked his manhood back inside his pants and then came forward with two other male vampires flanking him, perhaps in their early thirties.

The older-looking vampire yelled something to the others that sounded "screechy" and they all grew silent and turned to look at us. He walked forward, away from the other two males, and held his hands up and out to show he had nothing in them, although there were numerous automatic rifles in the room, including in the hands of the two male escorts.

"Lord DeRom, you bring us great honor in coming here!" He said in English, somewhat hissing his words. He had two large classic-looking vampire fangs in his oversized mouth that accounted for the hissing sound, as well as a tongue that must have been almost half a foot long and very thin and slender looking, almost as if it should be forked or something. It also seemed like it was covered with tough, hard-to-the-touch skin.

Lord DeRom placed his hand on my shoulder and I began reciting the words he was saying to me mentally, word-for-word. "I am pleased that you feel so, Falcon. I bring you greetings from the

Son Council."

"I send my greetings and respectful wishes back to the Council of the Sons. Have you any reply from them regarding the pleas we have made?" Falcon replied, his long greasy white hair hanging in his eyes.

He was wearing pants that I think were blue jeans at one time but were now so filthy and patched that they were unrecognizable. He also had a long brown leather trench coat filled with cuts and rips and some type of T-shirt on underneath it that revealed their unusual skeletal structure somewhat. They seemed to have extra ribs going lower down the stomach than a human did, as well as larger bones or something. They seemed to jut out more, which made them look rather boney. None of them were fat, and the girls could all easily have been models if they didn't have the unusual bone structure that was typical of the vampires in their true form, as well as the disgusting long tongues, pointed ears, and creepy glowing eyes. I imagined that if they resembled their vampire form in human form that, they would all be very good-looking people... albeit filthy.

Another thing I noticed was that they were all dressed pretty much in rags. None of them had two cents to rub together from the looks of it. Every article of clothing they had seemed to have been ripped and patched several times over.

Lord DeRom stepped forward and addressed them in Son in

his true voice. After every sentence, he would stop, and I would translate for him.

"Our Council regrets to inform you that we cannot in good faith, grant your request to formally support your cause. But while we will not back you in your fight, we will not give support them either. You are free to fight amongst yourselves. We do wish you well in your endeavor."

There were a few curses in the vampire language from the others, as well as a general look of defeat and angry despair. I hoped they weren't thinking about using their rifles... they had several.

Falcon closed his eyes and stared at the floor. He looked like he wanted to say something, a great many things actually, but he bit his tongue. When he looked up again, I could see tears in his eyes and I was surprised. I didn't think that a vampire would cry. It didn't seem to be something they could do. It floored me.

"So you are telling me that all whom I love are going to die." He said at last and Lord DeRom cocked his head sideways and looked at him curiously. He placed his hand on my shoulder and I heard his voice in my mind once again.

"No. I am telling you that the Son *Council* will not support either side. I said nothing of free-lance mercenaries."

Falcon looked at Lord DeRom curiously. So did I.

"You have likely heard of a group of Son females that have been causing problems for many years. They are a group of mostly V'Lin females called the "Sisters of Slaughter," and there are eight of them. They are a rogue faction, not supported by the Council. You will find them to be very disciplined and skilled in the art of combat. They are not under my control, nor are they sent on behalf of the Son or Alpha Council or people. They are acting on their own for payment. This, they say, they will take from your enemies. They have been notified of your need and will undoubtedly send someone to further negotiations. I can tell you with certainty that no other groups of my people will fight for your enemies at all."

Falcon looked at the others and shouted something in the vampire tongue and they all began to cheer. It was a very screechy-sounding language, almost like dragging nails across a chalkboard, but worse sounding. I could see the similarities to bats and I wondered if that was maybe where the whole bat concept came into play in popular vampire culture. I wasn't sure what he said to them, but they all seemed happy.

"Then this IS good news you bring us! The Sisters of Slaughter! Their mighty name has even made it to our meager hall... albeit in whispers. We will happily honor their requests for negotiations and we will let them take what loot they wish from our so-called leaders! We will also have a huge celebration once the battles are finished. I trust they will come to me in person to negotiate what their terms are in person?"

"Yes. They will arrange to come negotiate. The council does not object to you them working for you. They work on their own behalf. We are as one." Was the reply from Lord DeRom and he nodded to the vampires and then made to leave.

"Lord DeRom, I am pleased beyond words with the news you have brought us! We will celebrate! Surely you will join us? We do not have much, but we ask that you share in what we have, you and your... pet?" Falcon said, really noticing me for the first time since we arrived, only to call me a pet. It would prove interesting to see how the fierce V'Lin females dealt with them. The V'Lin are the most brutal of the Son's noble houses. They are radicals who hate anything not of their own culture and even many things that are. They are best described as a family of berserkers. They'd just as likely kill Falcon and his group as help them.

I expected him to say no and to just leave, but he conceded to staying and we returned to the center part of the cave. Once we were there, Falcon asked for permission to address me personally, which Lord DeRom granted.

I was leery of him, very leery, but he was polite, something I had not expected from a vampire. I still expected him to bite me at a moment's notice.

"My name is Falcon of the Taxiss Clan. I bid you welcome

to our humble dwelling. May I ask you some questions?" he said to me and I nodded my assent. He seemed to be very sincere.

"What is your name?" he asked and I felt kind of rude for not having offered it earlier. I had rather thought he would just sorta know or something.

"My name is Jackette MacNeill. I am Lord DeRom's Ally and Aide." I said to him, deciding that I could tell him the truth. I highly doubted that he would try anything against me, considering who my boss was.

"His Aide? Really? I am surprised. I did not know there were female Allies. Are you human or are you a mixed blood? Forgive me if I did not detect anything else from you. Son's and Alpha's are very hard for us to detect while in human form."

"I'm human. And yes, there are several female Allies." I told him and he nodded, letting it all sink in. He was really quite creepy looking, but strangely handsome all in one, sort of like a really cute corpse in bad need of a new wardrobe and a bath.

"Jackette, would you do us the honor of staying with us in celebration? I realize I had asked Lord DeRom, but not you. I must learn to see females as equals it appears... something highly uncommon for my kind. It will take some adjustment. I would also like to thank you for serving Lord DeRom so well. Your grasp of the Son language is flawless, from what little of it I know myself.

Another thing, do you know anything about these V'Lin females? They won't attempt to usurp our power when we are victorious, will they? I do not wish to exchange one group of dictators for another."

This was a question I did not know. I had only dealt with Lord DeRom and had no clue as to what the V'Lin females would do once they got here. They could very well eat the lot of them alive, roll around in their blood, and wear their skins for hats as far as I knew.

"I have never heard of the "Sisters of Slaughter" before. However, I do know quite a bit about the V'Lin. Mostly, I heard that they are very fierce in battle and very strict about Son laws in some ways, and yet they often blatantly violate them in others. I truthfully don't know if you can trust them or not. And as for staying for the celebration, yes, I accept and am honored to be invited. I thank you for personally inviting me." I said to him and he smiled. Seeing that oversized mouth full of tongue and fangs smile was far from reassuring.

"Very well then! Feel free to enjoy any of our luxuries we can offer! If you want to be bred by any of us, just approach us and ask. I'm afraid we have nothing that would serve as palatable human food or drink, though, but you are free to sample ours if you wish... I could have one of the others run up to the surface to buy something for you if you wish. We might be able to get some fine ramen noodles..."

"Uhhh... no thank you. I am on duty. I appreciate the offer though, and um... thank you for your generosity and hospitality. May I ask you a question, though, Falcon?" I said to him as graciously as I could. I knew that they obviously had little in the way of money and there was no way I was going to let them buy me something with what little they had. And I SURE as hell wasn't going to let one of those things take my virginity if I didn't have to.

"Yes, you may ask whatever you like." He replied, staring at me with those luminescent eyes of his. They were super light blue, like most of the other vampires, but I had seen other colors there, a light green, for example, and even one purple set on the girl that was giving him head earlier. They had really cool eyes. Creepy but cool.

"Where are we? What country is this?" I asked him simply.

He laughed. "Ah, so you came by portal! I have heard of them but my kind cannot open them. I *wondered* how you got through our security at the entrances. You are literally INSIDE the Emerald Isle Jackette. You are about half a hundred meters underneath Derry, Ireland. Have you travelled far through it?"

I blinked a few times, letting it sink in. With one step, I had crossed the Atlantic Ocean. It had taken, literally, a second or two. "We came from eastern Canada, a community called White River in a place called Prince Edward Island. Thank you." He left me then to return to the others.

I made my way back to Lord DeRom, who was standing between Falcon's two escorts, watching everyone intently. The two guards seemed nervous, and I wasn't sure what their duty was; to protect us from the others or to protect the others from us. I doubted they could do much to Lord DeRom if he wanted to do anything, though. All they had were rifles and the same fancy daggers that every vampire male warrior had that were made to identify the clan he belonged to. I wagered that Lord DeRom could tear them apart limb from limb in the blink of an eye if he so wished, rifles and fancy daggers meant nothing to him, not with mental abilities like his.

When I approached him, he touched my shoulder and I heard his voice enter my mind. "You do well, Ka'Dooog." That was all he said to me, but I felt an intense rush of satisfaction. Praise was said to be a rarity.

We stood there for a few minutes, just watching the vampires celebrating. Several of them approached us cautiously to ask us if we desired anything, and we always said the same thing: "Only to watch you rejoice."

Watching vampires rejoice is a scary thing... and very sexual. It seemed that the longer we stood there silently, the more and more they let down their guards and acted naturally. Couples joined from time to time to have intercourse, often with more than one partner, and they would even bite and drink each other's blood as they had sex. A few others danced, the females doing a strange belly dancing style of dance and the males performing a strange-looking step dance, according to whatever screechy tune played from the old ghetto blaster next. They also played a strange game of leaping over horizontal sticks, kind of like limbo, except instead of going under you went over, as well as games of kicking things held up higher and higher.

After about an hour of this, Lord DeRom decided that he had partied enough and that it was time to return home. He touched my shoulder and nodded at me, telling me it was time to go and to notify our two guards. I did so and one of them stepped up to Falcon, who was just finishing having another orgasm into the mouth of the same girl that had given him one earlier. He once again hastily pulled up his pants and jogged over to us. I had met him doing the same thing and I would leave him doing the same thing. It was kind of funny, in a way.

"Lord DeRom, Jackette, surely you are not leaving so soon? Are you sure I cannot get you something? You've enjoyed nothing we've had to offer." he said. I was flattered that he mentioned my name this time and never referred to me as a pet, at least.

"No. We enjoyed watching you rejoice. I am pleased that I came with good news." Lord DeRom said in Son which I translated for Falcon, then he spoke inside my head for me. "We must leave now, Ka'Dooog. Time waits for no one."

He spoke again in Son for me to translate to Falcon. "We offer thanks for allowing us to partake in your celebrations, as well as for your hospitality. We wish you luck in your endeavors. Farewell."

We walked back down the tunnel again and after we were out of sight, he re-opened the portal and a moment later, we were standing back in his back yard. I wasn't sure what time it was, but the sky was beginning to show signs of pre-dawn. He closed the portal and then turned to leave me. "Time to shift. I go now. Go home Ka'Dooog. You did well." He said as he started his walk towards the forest to shift.

"Thank you Lord DeRom. I was honored that you allowed me to go with you." I called out to him as he walked away. "What do I do with these robes I'm wearing?" I yelled out to him and he just waved his arm dismissively. "Keep. For next time." He said and then disappeared totally into the black.

I walked home. It was a nice night, I was full of energy, and the shoes were just SO comfortable it was hard to believe. "I was in Ireland! I went through a portal and in one second, I was in IRELAND! And I met vampires, real honest-to-God VAMPIRES! And I didn't puke! I thought for sure I was going to throw up that drink, but I didn't! I feel freakin' great!" I thought to myself as I walked. "Mom and Dad are gonna be so jealous!"

By the time I got home, it was almost daybreak. I got in the house and found Mom and Dad both sitting up at the kitchen table, waiting for me to come home. They both cried when they saw me come through the door.

"Oh thank God. Thank God..." was all Dad could say as he held me, sobbing like a baby, and Mom was all smiles and tears. "Oh Jackette! I'm so happy you got home safe and sound!"

I waited a few minutes until Dad finally contained himself. Seeing him tear up was a real rarity. Then the questions started.

"So what happened?" I expected this one. It was Mom who asked it.

"We went to Ireland to talk to a group of vampires," I said nonchalantly, smirking slightly. They were both crazy jealous.

"Ireland?! You went by portal? What's it like!?" Dad asked me excitedly. He was always fascinated by the portals.

"Weird... like walking through a doorway, really. You don't feel anything other than a weird pop in your ears... it sort of tingles a bit, too... I don't know if they all just go to the same place or if you have to use different ones for different places... or if they just make them wherever they want... but it's cool. It looks like heat waves, but there's no heat. Pretty much impossible to see through one, though, really super wavy looking. I couldn't really see anything till I was through." I told them both. They hung on every word, Dad especially.

"So you met vampires... not the 'be all, end all' the movies make them out to be, are they." Mom said to me and I shook my head in agreement.

"No, they aren't at all. They are faster than we are and stronger, they say, but a Son would rip them to shreds in seconds. They can supposedly drink a person dry of blood in a few minutes, though. These ones were nice enough, though, but Lord DeRom could have slaughtered them all with ease. They had guns, though, a lot of them. But they were glad to see us. He brought them good news. But yeah, they don't seem too tough. They were much nicer than I was expecting." I told them as Mom started to busy herself making breakfast. Dad was still hanging on every word.

"They didn't threaten you or anything, did they?" Dad asked me and I shook my head. "No. Not at all. Very polite and mannerly to us. We met with a guy called Falcon Taxiss. I didn't get the names of any of the other ones. There must have been twenty or more of them."

"Falcon. He's an assassin. Any of the vamps you meet named after a bird is an assassin. It's some sort of ranking system they have or something. Taxiss family. They were having issues a while back with their underlings. Their servants kind of rebelled against the higher ups in the family, demanding more rights and stuff. The vampires don't seem to have much in the way of a middle class. You are either crazy wealthy or dirt poor. The rich own the poor and made them work as slaves, basically. The Taxiss were some of the worst ones. Their leader is some old cheap bastard named Esau that is damn near a billionaire, while his people are starving to death. This revolt has been a long time coming in my opinion, but it's doomed. They'll never change anything." Dad told me when I was finished. I didn't know Dad knew so much about vampire politics, but then again, we were a member of the alliance for as long as I had been alive. He was bound to hear things.

"Dad, how come you and Mom were never more involved in the Alliance? I mean, you guys were in for years, and I was only in for a few, and I got to go do this stuff. Why?" I asked him and he shrugged.

"The Sons don't give their trust easily. Usually, Allies are kept at a distance for several generations before they are allowed to even *glimpse* a Son. To be taken on missions like you, that's usually only permitted for a person whose family has been in for seven or eight generations or so at the least… maybe even a dozen. You are an exception to the rule though because of being a Royal. He has you on all those diets and exercises for the very reason of being a low generation Ally. The Grands though take generations. Dozens."

"Generations? Good lord, why so long? Couldn't they find better Allies right off the street without waiting so long? Seems like a huge waste of resources to delay so long with getting Allies active." I said to him, feeling strange for being involved at the level I was now. Mom's family had been Allies for about three generations, or so I was told. Dad was a single generation. I guess that made me the fourth generation to be involved in a sense.

"They have a lot to risk by telling humans of their existence." Mom interjected as she cooked up pancakes. "They aren't scared of humans, though, I think they could likely win a war against us quite easily if they were to use some of the things I have heard they had. They have a lot of scary technology stored away that they could use against us. But they also have a lot of high end government ties, and not just one or two governments either. They don't want to rule us though... They want us to learn on our own. They are kind of forcing us to grow. They are more like teachers, I guess. The Sons are a strange breed."

I nodded. They were a strange breed of being. They had no desire to conquer humanity, or at least that was what I gathered from talking to Lord DeRom over the years. They could do some pretty amazing things, too, such as the portals and charming and whatever else they could do... But conquer all of humanity? I wasn't as sure as Mom was. The Sons may be impressive beings, able to do a lot of neat things, but there were only a few hundreds of them and eight billion of us.

Dad spoke up then. "I've heard of some of the Fets doing some freaky stuff... Just walk by and casually touching you and then have you drop dead a week later. And then they can "Charm," of course, and "Mask," which is sort of like "Charming," but it is done by a group of Sons, not just one, and basically renders them invisible. Then there is the "Dark Look" which is when they trigger the fear centers of your brain and implant a bunch of shit in there that drives you insane, and the "Brightest Needle" trick that allows them to find whatever they placed it on, sort of like a spirit tracking device, and other stuff that just freak me out... and then the technology they have... that's DAMN impressive too."

Mom nodded in understanding, but I was relatively lost. I had never heard of the tricks he mentioned other than charming, but I did know that Fet was a rank for top warrior. I assumed it was like a general or something. Technology? I didn't know they had much of it. From what I seen they seemed to be almost stone-aged in a lot of ways. The technology I had heard about was all Allied-made for them. When I said this to my parents, they shook their heads.

"Oh heck No. They have scads of technology. Crazy advanced, too. They say it isn't theirs, though. They say it was left here by "our parents." That other race, they say was around in Africa way back in the day. The O'Sian's." Dad said to me and my eyes grew large.

"So you're saying the O'Sian's are aliens? Or some race from the dinosaur times..." I said to him and he just shrugged.

"Yeah, I guess I am. I'm not sure which though." was all he said.

"Think we'll ever meet those guys? Are there any of them left?" I asked. He just shrugged.

"Shit... that'd be cool. Meeting somebody that is tougher than they are. Man, Lord DeRom seems... I dunno... NEAT!" I said at last and Mom laughed, Dad did too.

"Yeah, he's pretty interesting I'll give you that. He saved my bacon that time I fell through the ice. I was right under about four inches of it and he just smacked it with his hand and it shattered into a thousand little pieces. Damn, near popped my eardrums from the sound of it. I just remember seeing a blurry form through the ice over me and then the SMACK and I was being pulled out of the water. It was one hell of a blizzard that day. I was out in the smelt shack ice fishing and didn't notice the weather until it was time to go. My old ski-doo wouldn't start either, so I thought I'd risk it and walk home. I got lost out on the river and wandered around till it was good and dark and by then, I was just looking for shelter. Half froze, totally lost, and now miles from anywhere… I fell through someone's old fishing hole that was only a few inches thick and down I went. Drifted under the ice in the confusion and couldn't find my way out. He broke the ice, pulled me out, and the next thing I knew, I was at Rob's house, all warm and dry. I didn't remember any of it after being out of the water, he charmed me as soon as he got me out, except I remembered seeing the bottom of his feet from through the ice and I knew it was no human that pulled me out. It was him that introduced me to your mother actually, Rob, not Lord DeRom."

I had heard the story a few times but I always liked hearing it. The story Mom told me of how her great-grandfather became an Ally was even cooler, but it too involved the DeRom, except this time, it was Lord DeRom's aunt who had brought him in.

Apparently, my great-grandfather liked to drink a lot, and was often found drunk in the back of the wagon with the horse finding its own way home after he went to town. This was eighty or ninety years or more ago too, so cars still weren't as popular out where we lived and a few of the poorer folks still used horses. Anyhow, he had gotten drunk and let the horse walk home on its own with him in the back passed out, something he often did.

Well, apparently, one time a storm broke out and the horse got spooked by thunder or something and took off all willy-nilly with great-granddad still passed out in the back. It must have run way out through the countryside and got found by Lord DeRom's aunt Val who was locked in Son form her whole life. She found the horse and took it home, with great-granddad passed out in the back under a whole shit load of busted-up flour bags and busted molasses tubs. Anyhow, she didn't notice him until they were already at her little place and out of the storm. She was unhitching the horse when great-granddad stood up and then fell out of the back of the wagon, all covered in molasses and flour. I guess she nursed him back from the concussion he got falling out of the wagon and he became a member of the Alliance then and there. Got him off the sauce too.

"OK you two, time to eat." Mom announced as she began setting plates of pancakes down in front of us. "Time for talking later. Eat this, then go to bed. We could all use some sleep."

Chapter Four

Jesse

I awoke in the afternoon, showered, and got ready for what was left of the day. I sneezed and then took into a fit of coughing. "Great." I thought. I was coming down with a summer cold. I took some antibiotics to help nip it in the bud and then went downstairs to help Mom and Dad with the chores around the farm. That evening, after supper, I hopped on my bike and made my way to Rob's house, where I found him washing his old truck.

"Hey Jackette! How did it go last night?" he asked and I smiled. "It went well. We went to Ireland to talk to some vampires called the Taxiss. Man, they… Uh… Mate… A lot. Luckily, the girls can control their menstrual cycles or else there would be zillions of those guys around. They seem like ok folks, though."

He laughed. "Yeah, they have their moments. Grab a sponge and help me get this done, will ya?" he said, motioning to the truck. I obeyed and started washing while he disappeared into the house and reappeared with two beers, of which he gave me one.

"Here, drink this. You undoubtedly need it to get the taste of that shit he made you drink last night out of your mouth. Don't ya just love Son beverages? It'll either kill ya or cure ya... not much middle ground with those fellas. So. Now that you've met the big fella in the flesh. What do you think?"

"Oh damn, he's cool!" I said excitedly as I took the beer and drank a gulp of it. Beer was never my thing really, but it was cold and I was thirsty. "He's big... solid looking. How much does he weigh? Three hundred or so?"

"Two hundred and twenty-four pounds as of this morning, actually. He's a lot of lung and fur, remember." He said as he drank half his beer in one gulp.

"So he's the exact same weight as you are?" I asked him and he nodded. "They can't make mass out of something that isn't there. If I lost both my legs tomorrow and he shifted, he'd still have his legs, but the weight of them would be gone from his total mass, see? So he'd look really thin or shorter or something like that."

"Weird..." I said, thinking it over. "So theoretically, a crippled person could have a Son that can walk, right?"

"Right. Or a blind Host can have a Son that can see, etc. But it doesn't work the other way with the weight. If a Son loses his leg, we don't lose that mass or use of our leg, but it might feel funny or something from then on. A blind Son doesn't have a blind Host, though... Or vice versa. No abilities are lost, just mass, and only on them from us."

"I wonder how come?" I asked him and he shrugged. "I

dunno exactly. Probably something about being born in a human body. I think if I was born in a Son body and shifted into a human every so often, it would work the opposite way around, but that rarely happens. Pretty much all of us other than Alpha's are born in Human form to human parents."

"But it HAS happened... you did say *pretty* much." I replied, catching his uncertainty.

"Yeah, it has, a few times, but it's rare... really rare. Suppose a Son male met up with a Son female who was locked in form and either didn't have a human form or couldn't access her human form, and she got pregnant, she COULD give birth to a Son, a Human, or an Alpha... or possibly all three if she had triplets, but I doubt that'd happen. They would probably eat each other in the womb. That happens a bit."

"Ewww! Gross!" I said, grossed out at the thought of eating your twin in the womb. "That must make a lot of doctors freak out, wouldn't it? I mean, pretty much everybody now is born in a hospital. Heck, what about ultrasounds and stuff like that?"

"That's why we have Allies that work in delivery rooms as labor and delivery nurses and as ultrasound technicians and whatnot. We've carried out some amazing switches in hospital delivery rooms. That's why we need to have such a strict hold on all of our Allies and keep such meticulous records of Son's blood out there in case they get pregnant. I mean, nine times out of ten, they don't know about their Son heritage and the baby isn't a shifter anyhow, just a blood like them, but sometimes, the right combination happens and PRESTO! Bouncing baby shape shifter born to non-shifting, non-allied parents. It is not usually a problem until the kid is done growing its bones; we don't go through the first shift until we are usually late teens or early twenties, but still... sometimes stuff happens in the womb."

"Man, that must be weird. So last night, he mentioned something about the "Sisters of Slaughter" going to help the Taxiss vampires. What are they exactly? Mercenaries?"

He looked at me with surprise, not a good surprise. "The Sisters of Slaughter? They are a bunch of lunatics. Don't ever have anything to do with them. They are a group of radical Son female warriors that hate anything not Son. They are outcasts of Son society. They got booted out for being too sloppy. Throwing the rules of secrecy aside at every opportunity. They gave Lord DeRom a hard time a few years back, saying he was too passive with the humans and the vampires. They don't follow the treaty either... they go out in daytime, whatever they want. Total nut cases."

"What about their Host's?" I asked him and he just shook his head. "They shifted into Son form years ago and never shifted back. They hate humans, including their Host's. They are always trying some crazy stunt or another. Real hard asses. Always doing something stupid, putting us all at risk of getting noticed. Nothing more than a bunch of thugs for hire. Mercenaries are too kind a word for that bunch. The Vampires might regret becoming partners with them."

"So really, you guys really NEED the Alliance to help keep things secret," I said to him and he nodded, and then laughed.

"Yeah, we do. What, are you bucking for a raise or something?" he said and I chuckled and shook my head.

"No. Well, if you're offering, sure, but I'd really just like to do some more stuff like last night. That was awesome! How do the portals work? Does that one in the backyard just go to that place in Ireland where we went to last night?"

"No... they go all over the place for the most part. That one is partially locked here, but the other end of it is static and the Sons can control where they want it to go. There are loads of portals all over the planet, but only some of the Sons and a few other folks can access them to any degree of success. We can usually sense when we are near one, sometimes even call them to us." He told me as he continued cleaning the rims of his truck.

"The vampires can't use them, can they?" I asked and he shook his head. "Nope, the vamps have to fly in a plane like the rest of us. The portals are ancient in origin. O'Sian made originally... but only the Sons operate them with any success for the most part. It takes a special mind to get them open and to direct them, and humans or vampires just don't have it. Alpha's can't either. They can travel through them with a Son escort, but that's about it."

"So do they go anywhere else?" I asked him and he looked confused for a minute.

"You mean like off-world or something? You'd have to ask Lord DeRom that. I'm not entirely sure. I've heard rumors that the O'Sian's could go off-world with them. We can't." He told me as he finished with one rim and went to the next one.

We washed the rest of the truck in relative silence then, and when we were done, he asked me if I wanted to go for a drive with him. I piled into the passenger side and he got behind the wheel and started it up and we drove off towards the highway.

"Do you remember what he does when he's out? Can you access his memories and learn how to do stuff, like open portals?" I asked him and he shook his head.

"My mind is still a human mind for all intents and purposes. I know how to open a portal, I just physically can't. Remember now, Lord DeRom is a completely different person than me. Different minds and everything. He is not me in some other form. He's his own person completely, but we do influence each other. Think of us as roommates in the same space. Sometimes, he's in control of it, but most of the time, I am."

"That's so weird," I said and he laughed. "I mean, he could go out and get killed or something... what then? Would you die too? Without even knowing what happened?"

"Yeah, that's always a risk I take when I shift. I don't know if I'm going to be alive or not at the end of the night when there's a shift happening. I could die during the shift, which is always a very distinct possibility for me. Shifting is hard for us as a rule... and too damn hard for me. He's always had a problem with it. Some Sons do, some don't. It just happens that way. The luck of the draw, I suppose. My uncle could shift and still was able to walk at the same time. With me, it feels like my body is on fire and freezing at the same time and somebody is shattering all my bones with a hammer. Just kills me. Fifty-fifty chance of surviving each time."

"Man, that sucks," I said and he nodded his head and agreed, then resumed his driving in silence.

We drove for a few hours, just driving all around the western part of Prince Edward Island, where we called home, watching the sunset over the ocean as we went along the North Cape Coastal Drive in his old truck, going nowhere in particular.

He pulled into a takeout diner once we were almost home and asked me if I wanted anything to eat. I requested an ice cream and he disappeared inside to place the order while I sat in his truck and looked around at the other people there as well.

I spied some of the other people I went to high school with and one of them waved at me and came over, so I rolled down the window to talk to her. It was Shondra Jenkins, one of the sluttier girls around, but she was always friendly. A bit too-much-so most of the time.

"Jesse Williams has a crush on you." She told me point blank and I blinked and then laughed. Jesse Williams was the local heartthrob. He was also spent most of his time either playing hockey, in jail, or fishing lobsters, but almost always drunk or stoned. However, he was also a *very* good-looking guy and every girl in the area had a minor crush on him at one time or another, myself included. I just knew I could change him.

"Jesse Williams has a girlfriend, last I heard," I said to her and she shook her head no. "Nuh uh, he and Cheryl broke up." She said matter-of-factly. "Last week sometime."

"How did you know that he likes me? Did he tell you himself or something?" I asked, my mind racing. It was probably hearsay. Most of the rumors up here were that way. Somebody heard something and either got it all twisted around or just decided to lie about it and start rumors.

"Yes, I heard him say it to Chris Wallace down at the beach the other night. He said he seen you the other day and said you were looking good and that he was thinking about asking you out but thought you had a guy. You're not going out with HIM, are you?" she asked me, giggling, as Rob came out of the diner with my ice cream and a Styrofoam container of something for himself.

"Him? No! Gross! He's just a friend of my family. He's like forty-something!" I whispered to her as he approached the truck and passed my ice cream to me through the open driver's window before opening the door.

"So I'll tell him to call you then?" she said to me and I nodded. Jesse Williams was going to ask me out!

Rob looked at me and smiled as he pulled his truck out of the parking lot and back out onto the main road. "Who in the hell was that?" He asked me and I laughed.

"Shondra Jenkins. I went to school with her." I told him and he laughed.

"She sure likes to show her tits to the world. Looks like she was wearing her little sister's tank top." He said and I burst out laughing. Shondra was stacked and always wore clothes that showed off her boobs, although she probably shouldn't because she was getting to be a bit overweight and her shirts looked like they were about to explode.

"Maybe they're solar panels or something and she got to

make sure she gives them enough sun," I said and he burst out laughing again.

"Undressing her would be like opening up a bag of insulation". He said, making a zipper motion and then expanding his hands and I laughed harder than before.

We drove around for another half hour, driving through the small towns of our region, just talking about nothing in particular. It was a side of him I had rarely seen lately, just a laid-back, relaxed image of how he used to be when he was just the guy that lived down the road and not the Imperial Host.

"So what all was "Boobs" saying to you?" he said after a bit and I shook my head. "Oh, nothing, just that Jesse Williams supposedly likes me," I said nonchalantly. In truth it was all I could think about since Shondra had told me.

"Jesse Williams? The scuzzy little punk that's always in jail? I thought he was still behind bars for stealing catalytic converters from customer cars over at Paul's Muffler. Didn't he move to Summerside to leech off his poor mother? He's a little turd Jackette. You deserve someone better than that. Besides, isn't he with some other girl?"

I was mad at that but held my temper. "They broke up a few weeks ago. He's a nice guy." I said, not really believing it, but wanting to. He was a punk and he was always in trouble, but DAMN he was hot! He just needed a decent girl in his life, to help him out some. Cheryl was holding him back. I prayed that he would call me. I couldn't wait to go out with him!

We were near home now and he drove me the rest of the way in silence. "See ya, kiddo." He said to me as I got out in front of my house. "So I guess I'll see you Wednesday night then?"

"Yeah," I shot back. We usually always spoke to Lord DeRom on Wednesday night and I wasn't expecting anything else to happen then.

I shut the door with a casual goodbye and watched him as he pulled out of the laneway and drove down the road to where he lived. I couldn't quite see his house from our place, but he was the next house down our road, about a mile down. All that separated us were some trees, a few fields and a slight turn.

I went into the house and was greeted by Mom who told me that "Some guy had called." I checked the call display on our landline, angry that really active Allies like myself weren't usually allowed to carry cell phones for security reasons. I didn't recognize the number, but I called it. It was Jesse.

"Hey, Jackette? Jesse. What's up?" he said to me and I grinned excitedly.

"Not much. What's up with you?" I asked him back. He was

going to ask me out, I just knew it!

"I was wondering if you wanted to go to Summerside with me sometime, to catch a movie maybe, drive around a bit, you wanna go out with me sometime?" he asked me and I bit my hand in excitement. Every girl in the entire western part of the island wanted to date Jesse Williams.

"I guess so... sure," I said, trying to keep calm sounding on the phone. I thought I was gonna die.

"Cool. How about Wednesday night, then? I gotta work this weekend... pick you up at six." He said and then hung up. I screamed and jumped around for joy, then tore around my room like a maniac.

The rest of the week I floated on air. We had to work on getting in our winters wood that weekend, so we were all busy at that, with Dad and Rob cutting and Mom and I splitting and stacking in rows so it could dry out for the rest of the summer and fall before we threw it into our cellar.

Rob stayed to help out Monday and Tuesday as well, finishing up with all the splitting and stacking until it was completely finished. I had retired to the house, still battling my summer cold, pumping myself full of antibiotics and vitamin C, desperately trying to get rid of it before Wednesday. I would go regardless. I'd have to be in bad shape to cancel that date!

When six o'clock came on Wednesday, I was already standing by the door for almost half an hour. I told Mom to cancel my appointment with the Host for me cause I felt bad calling him up and doing it myself, and she frowned but then nodded. The last thing I wanted to hear was him harping on about how much of a dumb punk Jesse was and how I deserved so much better.

Jesse was late, ten minutes late, but that was fine because I had just finished touching up the finer points of my hair by then. I rushed out of the house without telling Mom and Dad much, other than "Going to the movies in Summerside with Jesse. Leave the door unlocked." After all, I was an adult, and I could do what I wanted.

Jesse and I didn't get there in time to go to the movies, but that was fine by me. We just drove around Summerside, then we drove out to the beach and Jesse parked the car and produced a four-pack of Bacardi coolers.

I drank the coolers while he smoked a joint and lit a fire. We laid down on a blanket talking and before long, we were making out. A few minutes later, he was on top of me, taking my virginity.

He wasn't gentle, but he wasn't rough either. I winced and endured losing my cherry to him. He came inside me after a few painful minutes and then pulled out of me and laid next to me on the blanket, panting.

"I was wanting to do that to you since I saw you at the beach this summer." He said to me and then reached for another joint. He offered it to me after he had it lit, but I refused it with a frown. Smoking was gross and forbidden. If you wanted to be an Ally, you couldn't smoke, especially a mind-altering drug. The vampires were the same way. Anything that made you mentally altered was seen as weak and was outlawed, basically. Recreational drugs, smoking, and even drinking to excess. Even putting on too much weight was not allowed. It was seen as a lack of self-control.

"That was my first time," I told him and he laughed. "Really? Cool." He said and then sucked on his joint and then blew out a smoke ring.

"Want another cooler?" he said to me, popping the top off of one and taking a drink of it before offering it to me. I accepted it silently and laid there looking up at the stars and the way the smoke from our fire and his weed rose up to meet them together, entwining together as one as the heat from the blaze drew it upwards.

A few minutes later, he finished his joint and tossed it in the sand and then he started kissing me and then got on top of me once again.

He had his way with me again and after a few more minutes of sex, he finished and pulled his pants back on. "Getting late, better get you home," he said after looking at his watch. "Besides, I gotta work tomorrow."

I gathered up my clothes after washing myself off in the water slightly. It was now late summer and the water was getting too cold for swimming in. I hurriedly got dressed and went back to his car, where he was waiting for me with the engine running.

He sang a song he wrote for me on the way home. It wasn't great, neither was his singing, but I loved the thought that he had written it for me. I grabbed my leftover pop that we had gotten at a local burger place and swished my mouth out to get the taste of his marijuana breath out, then spit it out the window.

He dropped me off at the house and I hobbled up to my room, sore as hell from losing my virginity. The alcohol was wearing off and the pain was coming now. I swallowed a few Advil, popped a few more antibiotics, took a shower, then hit the bed and was asleep before my head hit the pillow.

I awoke the next morning to Dad vacuuming the upstairs hallway. I crawled out of the bed and felt my head and vagina throbbing. I reached for more painkillers, the last of the antibiotics, and a birth control pill, swallowed them all at once, and then drank the large glass of water sitting next to them that I had the wisdom to place there the night before. I was just glad that my cold seemed to be pretty much finished.

I got up after a few minutes and cleaned up for the day and hid my pain as I made my way slowly downstairs. Mom was in the kitchen but had her back to me as I entered and when she turned around, I was already sitting.

"Good morning! Have fun last night?" She asked me and I nodded with a smile. "Had a blast!" I said to her and then thought slyly. "Had sex on the beach *twice* with Jesse Williams in Summerside! I had a ball... two, actually." I said silently in my mind with a giggle.

"Where did you go? It would have been too late to see a movie by the time you left last night." She asked me as she motioned for me to eat some of the pancakes she had sitting on a plate.

"Yeah, we got there ten minutes too late to see it so we just drove around mostly. Went to a beach party out at Chelton beach for a bit." I said, not really lying. It was a party on the beach, just for the two of us.

"Who did you go with? I've seen that car around town before, but I was never sure who owned it."

"Jesse Williams," I said calmly. Mom knew I had a crush on him for a while.

"The boy you were all crazy over? He's a lot older than you, isn't he? The hockey player?"

"Yeah, he's not so much older. He's still in his twenties... I think." I said to her, wondering just how old Jesse was exactly. He wasn't in school with me. I had heard he had quit. I thought he was still in his late twenties... I wasn't sure, though.

"So, did it go well? He going to ask you out again?" She asked me and I shrugged then nodded with a grin.

"Yeah, I imagine he will. We had a lot of fun last night." I said, smiling to myself.

Dad came in then and the conversation about Jesse was dropped and switched over to the new hydraulic pump we needed for the tractor. I was glad.

That afternoon I hung around the house, still a bit sore from last night's encounter, and waiting for Jesse to call to see about another date. Days passed and nothing, then he called me on Monday asking me out for Wednesday again. I told Mom to tell Rob I wouldn't be by again tonight, but maybe tomorrow night would be better.

Jesse and I went for another drive down to Summerside, and after a few trips through town and a stop at the burger place's drive-thru, we were back at our spot on the beach and naked on our big towel.

It hurt like hell doing it sober, but I welcomed him between my thighs eagerly. This was it, I thought. He's gonna ask me to be his girlfriend tonight!

He didn't ask me to be his girlfriend, though. He did say that he worked a lot and that he'd like to see me next Wednesday as well, but that was it when it came to a commitment of any sort. He wouldn't even go with me to the mall or into any of the restaurants to eat, saying he hated eating in them. He wouldn't even go to the clubs for a beer, saying he didn't like them 'cause everybody just wanted to fight all the time. I didn't doubt it. All the guys envied him.

The next morning, I slept in late again, then went out to help with my chores around the farm. I was still a bit sore from having sex with Jesse, but the pain just made me smile when I thought about it. The pleasure was better than the pain. It would only get better in time.

Later that evening, I called up Rob.

"Hey, how's it going?" I asked him as he picked up the phone and said hello.

"Good, good. How are things with you? Missed you the other night." he said back.

"Yeah, I was out on a date. Went down to Summerside for a drive."

"Yeah? What's all new in Summerside? Been a few weeks since I was there."

"Not much. Same old, same old." I said to him. "Any news from Lord DeRom?"

"Wouldn't know." He told me. They didn't really communicate overly well... or often. "He is stirring around a bit in there, though... probably 'because you never showed up. He's just wondering what's going on. He's big on patterns."

"Yeah, sorry. I had a bad cold. It's just clearing up now. When would be good to talk then?"

"Not sure... tonight maybe, if you want? Not much else going on with me. Good for you?"

"Sure, why not?" I said and he agreed to tonight and then said his farewells and hung up.

I set the phone down and Mom looked at me, who had just come into the room.

"Who was that?" She asked and I nodded my head towards Rob's house and she nodded in understanding. "Going over tonight to talk."

"Good. Find out when a good time for me and your father to go talk to him too. It's been a while. Hey now, think he'd mind if we went tonight, too? Two talks at once. Make things easier for him, undoubtedly."

I shrugged. "Can't see it mattering," I said and picked up the phone to re-call him and ask.

He told me he didn't mind if Mom and Dad came too and that evening, we all showed up at his house. We all just sat around his living room talking nonchalantly, when Mom asked him a question, I was kind of wondering myself.

"How old are you now? You have a birthday in October, don't you?" she said to him and he nodded.

"I'll be thirty-five." He said and I cocked my head. Thirty-five? Really? I had thought that he was a lot older for some reason. He didn't look old or anything, he just seemed to be older. I guess it was because he had always been around our place when I was growing up. I just assumed he was older. Not many guys at thirty-five live alone in an old farmhouse and have been doing so for as long as he had been. He must have been alone over there for almost twenty years. Nobody else had ever lived there as long as I could remember.

"Do you want us to throw you a little get-together?" Mom asked and he looked at her like she was nuts and then shook his head. "No thanks, Baby. I'll pass on the parties. I'm the wrong kind of animal. I'm a strange animal, but you're looking for a party animal," he said and we all chuckled.

"Well, we should get talking. He'll be long-winded with the three of you here. Don't let him go on too long, ok? I would like to get up before noon tomorrow.”

A few minutes later, we were ready to start. We were all sitting on the floor of his bedroom and he was perched on the bed. Dressed in a pair of jogging pants and covered with his purple silk sheet. A stick of incense smoldered nearby and the room was darkened and soft new aged Celtic music played on the stereo in the corner at a low volume. Lord DeRom didn't care much for most human music, but some of it he really liked. The Celtic New Age genre seemed to be his favorite, as long as there were no words. Rob stared at the incense ember for several minutes, slowly bringing Lord DeRom to the surface and before long, his head dropped and the breathing started to deepen and we knew Lord DeRom was coming out.

“Greetings,” he said, crossing his arms and bowing like he usually did. His eyes were closed and the pinky fingers were curled over the middle fingers as usual.

“Greetings, Lord DeRom,” Mom said since she was the eldest Ally here. It was always the highest ranking Allies duty to do the initial greeting during a talk, and Mom was it.

“Ah... Eliza and Steven... and Ka'Dooog. It has been a while since we all spoke together.”

“Yes, yes it has.” Mom said in agreement. “Was there anything you wished us to do for you, my Lord?” She asked and he nodded.

"Yes... I will be needing assistance again. Ka'Dooog, will you serve me once more?" he asked. I eagerly jumped at the opportunity. "Yes! Yes I will! When and where will I be going?"

He looked at me strangely, well, as strangely as one could with his eyes shut. He rarely opened his eyes when we spoke to him like this. He disliked the confusion of seeing through human eyes. Rob had often said that Lord DeRom would get somewhat envious of the human ability to see such vibrant colors than he could see in Son form.

"Jackette... you will be unable to serve me then." He said to me oddly, his head cocked to the side. He looked very confused. He was also sniffing the air near me slightly. I looked at Mom and Dad curiously and then at Lord DeRom.

"Why will I be unable to serve you then?" I asked him and he looked dead at me with his closed eyes like he could see through his eyelids or something.

"Because I will need an Aide in four months for a talk, but you will be getting heavy with your child then." He said to me and I gasped, albeit not as loudly or as sharply as Mom and Dad did.

"With child?" I said and he nodded and pointed at my belly. "Yes. With that child. It is new in you, but it grows even now. I can feel its energy." He said and I shook my head. It was impossible, I thought! Sure, I had unprotected sex, but it was only a few times, and I was on the pill!

"Lord DeRom, we need to talk to Jackette about this. We did not know this information." Dad said to him and Lord DeRom nodded in understanding and then brought Rob back out.

"So... that was quick," Rob said cheerfully as he noticed the clock. It had only been a few minutes. "Everything O.K?"

"Yeah, we have something of a family emergency right now... sorry about this." Dad said as he got up and flicked on the lights, making us all squint with the sudden change from soft mellow lighting to the harshness of electric light.

"Anything I can do?" Rob yelled out as we all made our way downstairs and then out the door. I was in tears and Dad was furious. Mom was just silent, and I think that scared me more.

That night, I told them what had happened with Jesse. Not all the gory details, mind you, just that we had had sex a few times and I couldn't figure out how I had gotten pregnant if in fact, I was.

"I know." Mom said. "You were taking antibiotics. Sometimes, that will negate the pill."

I nodded. I had taken antibiotics for the summer cold I had. I never thought anything about them after that, either. Just great. So much for being considered the smart one of the family.

"So... What are you going to do?" Mom asked me and I shrugged. What options did I have? Be a single parent? Abortion? Adoption? Marriage? I would jump at the chance of being married to Jesse. He was just so awesome! I knew he was going to do the right thing once he found out... I just knew it!

"I'll tell Jesse... and we'll figure it out from there." I said to them and they nodded quietly in acceptance. Dad was upset... highly upset... but what else could I do? I felt bad for making him feel like this, but there was little I could do about it now.

Jesse called a few times throughout the week to see if I was available for Wednesday night again, but I told him I wasn't feeling well. After a few weeks, I decided to call him and tell him the news to see what he thought of the whole thing.

"Hey baby. I was just gonna see if you wanted to go for a drive." He said to me and I told him I had to talk to him. "Sure," I said to him. I figured it would be a good time to get a chance to talk to him... Tell him the news. "Great. I'll pick you up in an hour." He told me and then hung up.

An hour later, Jesse pulled into the laneway. I noticed Dad getting up and going to his gun closet for his shotgun, but I stopped him. "Dad, it's just as much my fault as it is his," I said to him and he bit his lip and then went back to his chair. Dad was quiet a lot lately... and I knew he was very upset about my situation.

I ran out to the car and quickly jumped in and Jesse turned and then drove out the laneway. He kissed me briefly on the lips, then undid his zipper and gave my head a push for me to go down on him as soon as we were out of the laneway. "No... I have to tell you something." I said to him and he looked annoyed.

"What's wrong Jackette?" he said.

"I'm pregnant," I replied bluntly and he looked at me with a grin. "Really? Is it mine?" He said and I nodded, feeling degraded by his comment. "You were the only guy I was with, Jesse. I told you that."

"Cool. Yeah, just checking. So what are you gonna do?" he said to me with a slightly drunken slur. He was drinking... or something. It was a usual state to find him in.

"Well, I was wondering what YOU were gonna do. I think we should get married." I said to him and he laughed and pulled the car over to the side of the road.

"Married? Are you for real?" he said to me and then laughed. "I ain't marrying you! I have a fiancé already."

My gut rolled over and I blinked back tears. I was reeling in shock. "A fiancé!? Who? Since when?" I screamed at him. He just laughed.

"Cheryl, since last year sometime. Why?" he said and I started to cry. He had used me like everyone said he does to girls. I hadn't wanted to believe the rumors, but this was no rumor. My belly would soon be proof of that.

"But... you said you were single!" I said to him between sobs. He shook his head.

"I never said that at all. That was Shondra saying that. Cheryl and I broke up for a bit, but we're back together. She knows I have other girls, though. She doesn't care."

I was numb. "Other girls? How many other girls?" I asked him and he shrugged and grinned smugly.

"Five other ones, other than you and her." He said. He had one for every day of the week, the bastard. It all made sense now, I was his Wednesday night fling.

"Well then, how many of them are carrying your child?" I said, crying now. My heart was shattered and I was furious at him, and myself for being so stupid.

"I dunno... I have a few out there now, I guess." He said and I knew that he had no cares at all about leaving a wake of bastards in his trail. The rumors were right and I was an idiot for not listening to them.

I sobbed hard then, and I could feel him turn the car around and take me back home. I had my head buried in my hands and I was totally out of it for the most part. I barely remember him stopping the car and getting out and opening my door. He led me out of his car and I started freaking out at him, slapping and punching him. I was pretty sure he was laughing at one point, but not when I heard Dad's voice and then a shotgun blast.

"Jesus!" Jesse squealed as Dad's blast splattered pellets all through the passenger side front fender of his beloved Cutlass Supreme. Jesse ran around to get back in his car and tore out of the laneway, spraying me and everything else nearby with laneway gravel. I didn't feel it. I only felt pain inside me at being used like I had been. I was such an idiot.

I felt Mom's arms wrap around me and she led me to the house, where I collapsed on the floor of the porch in a sobbing heap. Dad and Mom carried me upstairs to my room and put me to bed and I spent the night there, screaming into my pillow and hating myself now and the life growing inside my body.

I thought long and hard about abortion, but just couldn't do it. I had no ill towards anyone who did decide to do it, I was pro-choice, but I just didn't feel that it was the right choice for me. It wasn't the baby's fault, it was mine and Jesse's.

The situation resolved itself a week later when I miscarried. I was a total wreck for weeks, feeling shame and guilt and anger at myself and Jesse, but mostly at myself. Jesse had simply done what I allowed him to do. I was the idiot. He was a piece of shit, mind you, a complete-and-total, no-parts-missing piece of shit... But I was the idiot.

The Alliance became my whole life then. The real world was a waste of time. It was evil and stupid and I found it just to be so "common". I had heard Lord DeRom and Rob both refer to non-allied humans as "the common herd" and always thought of it as a derogatory term and somewhat insulting, but it wasn't. It was just stating a fact. They WERE common, they WERE herd-like, and I wanted as little to do with them as I could. I just wanted to do Allied things and make a difference in the world from the silent sidelines.

And then one day, I got my wish.

Chapter Five

Natasha

It had started off innocently enough. We were talking to Lord DeRom and I was informed that he needed a spy. I asked for what and he said for a secret mission on the Grand Alliance, the branch of the Alliance that dealt with the day-to-day operation of Son secrecy and dealings.

I went ballistic with joy then. I had always wanted to be more involved and this was a perfect opportunity. When I asked why he chose me, he told me that it was because I was a Royal Ally that had made me perfect for the job. The Grand Allies were all well known to the Alliance, but Royal ones were not. Lord DeRom never told any of the Grand Alliance members about having his own Royal Alliance, except for a few very high-level members, and this made us very good people to monitor most of the Grand Alliance's activities from within.

I was sent out of province then, out to Manitoba, where I was recommended by one of Lord DeRom's Grand Alliance contacts to work at a place called "Allied Holdings." Officially and on the records, Allied Holdings was a warehousing company for other businesses. In actuality, it was a place where the Alliance kept their technology, researched it, and developed uses of some of it for human use. They kept stockpiles of the technology the Sons and

Alphas were entrusted with by the O'Sian's, but these materials were finding their way into other people's hands as of late and I was sent to find the leak. Other people were sent to do it as well, Grand Alliance members, and I was contacted shortly after landing in Manitoba by people Lord DeRom had informed would be meeting me. I was to tell none of them I was a Royal Ally. To them, I was simply the daughter of a mid-level Grand Ally.

Apparently several discoveries in the computer and scientific fields that humanity had achieved lately were of O'Sian design and were not supposed to have been released to mankind yet. He wanted to find out how that was happening, so I was sent with some others to infiltrate "Allied Holdings" and find out if there was a rat in the wolf den, as it were.

None of the others knew I was fluent in the Son language. As far as anyone was told, I didn't work for the DeRom or even know of them, and I was to act as green as could be, and to monitor the foreman to see if he was involved with the missing technical information. If he was, we were to inform our superiors at once and await further orders.

As I had said, Lord DeRom also had a few other individuals working undercover at "Allied Holdings" to see if the rat could be caught. As far as the Grands were concerned, most of them had only briefly HEARD of the DeRom family as a ruling class, and much of

Son culture was kept from them if they were lower generations so as not to be a security risk.

These higher generational Allies had dealings with Son Host's and Alpha's on an almost daily basis, but it was a one way relationship for the most part. They were told what to do by the Son's and Alpha's and they did it. There was little discussions about anything other than the task at hand. I would know more about the finer workings of Son culture than the lot of them combined.

My boss's name was Mr. Alan Matsufuji, a half-Japanese, half-Caucasian man in his mid-sixties. He was also one of the prime suspects in the smuggling of Son tech as well, or so I was told. I was hired to be his assistant secretary of sorts and to report back any news to Rob to give to Lord DeRom. I looked forward to it.

One of the other Allies sent to spy with me was Natasha Olegaard and she was from somewhere in Eastern Europe. The Grand Alliance had sent her to work in Canada with a visitor's visa. She was about my age, early twenties, and she was exceptionally beautiful. She had long, platinum-blonde hair, stunning body, and piercing blue eyes. Every guy that seen her was gaga over her, and I felt somewhat jealous of her. I found out that she was part vampire, which explained a lot in regards to her looks and sex appeal.

"My mother was a member of a religious Sept that was monitoring vampire activity, but she was raped by a vampire while working undercover. I was the result." She told in her thickly accented voice one day over lunch. She had told me to point blank while we were outside on a bench under an old pine tree, eating sandwiches and drinking lattes from the neighboring little coffee shop. Natasha and I had become very close friends.

"Oh my God, that's awful!" I told her and she nodded. "She would have aborted me, she told me, but she was working undercover and couldn't blow her cover. Now, that is what I call dedication." She said of her mother and I nodded and immediately thought of the miscarriage I had had earlier.

"Do you find there to be a lot of suspicion of the Sons to where your loyalties lie?" I asked her and she nodded.

"There used to be... yes... until I bring to them my father's head. After that, I was accepted completely." She said and I gasped.

"You killed him?! Good for you, but... how? Wasn't it hard?" I asked her and she nodded after some thought.

"Yes, it was. Vampires are very strong compared to humans, but if you are smart it is not difficult at all. They are very fond of drinking alcohol to excess and sex, much like human men. I got myself involved with a vampire group on the computer and searched through for actual vampires, not just the wannabes. For every one hundred wannabe vampires and role-playing fools out there, there are one or two true vampires keeping an eye on things from the shadows, seeking out people they figure would be good Allies to have, or victims. I made my online image look to be a very good target for being in their Alliance; compliant, attractive, and with no close relatives. I got accepted in, and made my acquaintance to my father's clan as fast as possible.

After a few weeks, I met up with him. I allowed him to seduce me, and I invited him to my place. Alcohol doesn't work well on me or most mind-altering drugs. It is a trait that happens sometimes with hybrids like me. Anyhow, after he drank a few bottles of wine and was tired out from sex, I drove a knife into his neck as he slept. I told him who I was before he died, then I took his head to the Alliance and they never gave me a hard time again, or allowed anyone else to either."

My eyes were wide as Natasha told me her story. I had no idea how she could have done it, had sex with a vampire, her own father nonetheless, and then cut his head off. I hadn't killed anything in my life, not even chickens back on the farm. I had run over a cat once with the tractor and had sobbed myself to sleep for days afterwards. I didn't think I could kill a person, no matter what they had done to me. Not even Jesse.

The next week, Natasha told me that she had thoroughly investigated Matsufuji and found him to be relatively honest. A few minor indiscretions, nothing major though, and nothing that would interfere with Son activity. It was time for us to change departments.

She was then sent to work in accounting and I was shuffled off down to records. Both areas were potentially good areas to find trouble, but after a few more months of dutiful spying, nothing was found and we were shuffled again.

This time, Natasha was sent to shipping and I was sent to maintenance, and we both made discoveries that made the Alliance wonder.

Natasha had discovered that numerous trucks were coming and going from the warehouse without anyone listing them. Inventories were off or modified, and bills of lading for shipments were modified as well. Truckloads of equipment were being sent out and received without any records being kept, and Natasha began to monitor her foreman, Mr. Wayne Bulmer, very closely.

The discovery I had made was that the blueprints for the building showed that there were one hundred and forty-three electronic doors in the main "Allied Holdings" building, but in fact, there were one hundred and forty-four. I know, because I counted each and every door... four times just to be sure. To be honest though, the one door that I found was *not* supposed to be found. It was on the shipping elevator's floor and with some more snooping through the blueprints, I discovered that it led to a secret area underneath the main complex itself that had been added during Mr.

Bulmer's scheduled times and was listed as septic and structural work but was in fact not.

Natasha and I compared notes and we recognized that the trucks she had noticed all routed equipment through the same cargo elevator I had discovered to have a door on the bottom of it. We also discovered that Mr. Bulmer had a brother-in-law working there, Mr. Eric Stotski, who was ironically, one of the maintenance men, specializing in, you guessed it, elevators. He also had a construction business, which specialized in cement basements and septic lines. Under careful scrutiny, we discovered that it was his company that had installed the secret chamber.

We managed to sneak a small motion-sensitive camera into the elevator and aimed it at the keypad so we could figure out how they were accessing the door to get into the secret area. After a few days of monitoring and placing dozens of small cameras everywhere, we seen Mr. Stotski go into the elevator, hit the basement key, hold it in, then hit the roof-level key twice. The floor of the elevator opened and lowered to another level. The camera could only show so much, having been aimed at the keypad and not the floor, but we did see a forklift come and retrieve the load he had taken in, and replace it with a different one. He rose back up in the elevator again, this time with his new load, and was on his merry way.

When we told this news to our superiors, it was well received.

"A secret level accessed under the floor of the shipping elevator? Genius!" The Allied contact named Tristan Dumas that we were reporting to had said to us. He was a member of the Wara Clan, a conglomeration of black-furred families that tended to work in military and security. "We need to find out where this goes. We will monitor both Mr. Stotski and Mr. Bulmer and find out what's going on. We'll watch them until we find out where they are sending the stuff to. You two have done splendidly. I'm very impressed with your work. I'll mention you both to my superiors."

Natasha and I both blushed from the praise of Mr. Dumas and then I asked, "So what do we do now? Are we done or what?"

Our superior nodded. "Yes. We'll deal with Stotski and Bulmer and you two can return home. You won't want to see what's going to happen to them. My people don't take greed or theft lightly. This technology shouldn't have been released for another decade."

I smiled broadly and thanked him. Natasha was quiet, but smiled. When our superior had left, I asked Natasha what was wrong.

"Oh, it is nothing. I just enjoyed working with you and being here in Canada. I have no real place to go. My mother had been dead for some time now and I have no siblings or relations. You are as much family as anyone. I have no real reason to go back home to Belarus." She said glumly. She had said before that she had nobody back home, I just didn't realize that she didn't want to go home at all. I thought for a second, then hugged her.

"Well, you can come home with me. We have lots of room at my parent's place if you don't mind helping out with the farm."

She looked at me curiously and then smiled. "Farming? I know nothing about farming... but I can learn! Are you certain your parents would not mind? It is too much to ask. I would hate to impose."

"They won't mind. And if you want you could always get a job somewhere so you could stay in Canada. We'll help you get settled into the country if you want to stay." I said to her excitedly. I liked the idea of Natasha being around all the time. She had become my best friend.

She nodded and then giggled excitedly. I phoned Mom and Dad and told them I was coming home and bringing a friend and Dad drove to the airport in Charlottetown to meet us when we had returned from Winnipeg.

Dad's eyes nearly popped out of his head when he seen Natasha and I chuckled. She sat between him and me in our truck on the way home from the airport and I noticed that he kept peeking at her in the rearview mirror. It was impossible not to. She was utterly gorgeous. It had been almost annoying at the airport, every sleazy guy in the place was coming up to her to talk. I just hoped that Dad wouldn't try anything stupid.

Natasha told us her story once again over a hot bowl of Mom's clam chowder when we finally got home, and Mom and Dad were totally enthralled by her tale of sadness and savagery. When she went to the shower, Mom, Dad and I all sat around to talk.

"She can stay here as long as she likes." Mom and Dad both said together. I figured they would have no issues with me bringing her home, I was glad I was right.

"Should we tell her that we are Royal Allies, and not just Grands?" I asked them and they grimaced.

"She doesn't know already?" Mom asked and I shook my head no. As far as Natasha knew, I was just another Grand Ally, like her.

"We'll have to talk to Lord DeRom about this, or Rob at least. I don't want to bring in new Allies without his say. That happened before years ago and it failed miserably. I'd hate to see him have to do anything to her because we jumped to conclusions and made assumptions." Dad said and Mom nodded in agreement. I nodded as well. I wanted Natasha to be my friend and to become a Canadian, not to become one of Lord DeRom's victims.

The next day Natasha and I went out to explore the farm while Dad and Mom went to Rob's house to discuss matters with him. That evening he arrived at the house and we all sat down and he told Natasha who and what he was. It went over relatively well, considering.

"You are the Host of a DeRom? THE DeRom?" she gasped after a bit and he nodded. "I like to keep a relatively low profile, as does Lord DeRom. I maintain a small personal alliance made up of people I trust, and very few others know I am here. I prefer to keep it that way, too." He said to her and she nodded, catching the hint.

"I wouldn't dare mention a word of this to anyone else. But my Lord, why have you allowed me? I mean, I am... a half-breed." She said softly and my mind went to racing. She WAS a half-breed, after all. What if she could control minds or something? Vampires did have a limited ability for that stuff. They could sometimes affect minds. Amplify weaknesses and whatnot in weaker-minded humans. Sometimes, even make friends turn on one another if they want to cause turmoil, things like that. Maybe she had been playing me? Could she play him too?

"I see no reason not to trust you because you are half vampire. I know your history. I have spoken to others about you, others you know and who know you well, including some you don't know who know you well. All say you are trustworthy, and I can tell that you would not be a traitor. You have served the Grand Alliance loyally, now I ask that you leave the Grand Alliance to serve the Royal Alliance just as loyally." He said to her and she began to mist up around the eyes and nod. She bowed to him and he just laughed and then hugged her. "We're not overly big on formality here. Welcome to our merry band of misfits."

The rest of the evening went by leisurely, with Rob staying and answering loads of questions from Natasha. It really got interesting when she asked him when he got into the Alliance, and if he had always known what he was.

"No." He said and it shocked me. "My father was the Host of Gran'Dee DeRom. I also had four uncles and an aunt who shifted, as well as a cousin whose partially mind shifted. Yo'Nuk, Ho'Mus, Al'Ladir, and Gar'Maz'De were the uncles, with Ho'Mus being the real force behind the throne as it were, and my cousin Alfred, who partially shifted, who carried the Son named Nee'di'am. As for Aunt Val, well, she was always in Son form. She never married or had any offspring. Uncle Yo'Nuk was insane by all standards. He had a condition known as "Farrakis" or "The Hunger", which made him crave human flesh. He never acted on it, but damn near did a few times. He passed away a few years ago. None of his children ever did breed true enough to have a shifter, though... 'cause his wife was of low blood. As for Ho'Mus and Gar'Maz'De, well, they never had kids. That's a long story. A real strange and sad tale, that is..."

"What happened?" Dad asked him and he looked up and smiled sadly at us.

"Oh, the usual thing that happens to the DeRom and their Host's. We die alone, you know. Usually live alone, too. Anyhow, every so often, one of us gets a chance at love. Sometimes, it works out, other times, well... It just doesn't. Ho'Mus was to be married through an arranged marriage to a lady who was a Son as well. Anyhow, she came to stay with our family years ago, long before I was born, and she fell in love with my OTHER uncle, who was the Host of Gar'Maz'De. They had an affair in human form, and once Gar'Maz'De heard of it, he was so angry at her that he killed her. His Host was so overcome with rage towards him that he killed Gar'Maz'De by bringing him forth while intoxicated, then staying that way for the rest of his life for the most part. Gar'Maz'De warped his body as he died, as revenge, turned him into a hunchback, and my uncle was left a bitter, sad, lonely old alcoholic. The lady was buried secretly by Gar'Maz'De somewhere out back of our land, and Ho'Mus never allowed his Host to know what had happened, so as to keep the peace between the two brothers. As far as the Host of Ho'Mus knew, she just ran away one day. Her spirit still roams the grounds sometimes, always in the late fall, during the windiest and rainiest times. I've heard her crying a few times... it's very unsettling."

We were all spell-bound then and he looked at us all and

chuckled. "What?" he said to us and shrugged. "We have our romance stories too, ya know."

"So you're saying there are ghosts in the woods too?" I said to him and he nodded. "One at least... that I've seen anyways. Probably more. Lord knows there are enough bodies scattered around out there to have more than one ghost." He said and I blinked.

"Dead bodies? How many dead bodies are there here?" I asked and he laughed. "Well, put it this way, if all the dead people that were buried out there suddenly popped up out of the ground, there'd be a heck of an overpopulation issue going on in town."

"Really? You guys killed that many people?" I said and he looked at me and I felt a pang of regret go through me as soon as I said it.

"Not just us, although we have killed a few. It wasn't all murders, either. We've had a few suicides happen back there, a few sick, some of old age. But as for murder, humans killing humans have been the main contenders for that, my dear. Gar'Maz'De killed his brother's fiancé, Yo'Nuk didn't kill anyone as far as I know, nor did Need'iam or Gran'Dee. Ho'mus' Host killed a man, though, during the depression. Some guy had snuck onto our property and had found Aunt Val, who was deathly ill at the time and unable to defend herself. My uncle pitchforked the guy through the chest before he attacked her."

"I don't blame him then," Dad said and we all nodded. I could agree with that. He was defending his sister, really.

"What about you?" Natasha asked and he grew silent. We all did. I had no idea if he had ever killed anyone. I didn't know if I wanted to know.

"Yes. I did kill once, but Lord DeRom has killed more than once. The man I killed was a Grand Ally who thought he could come here and extort us. Lord DeRom killed several men, one who was out jacking deer in New Brunswick who had shot him just after shifting, and three vampire allies up in Northern Ontario who had kidnapped a teenage native girl and who were raping her in some little hunting shack-up near Espanola. I'm not sure how many vampires he killed over the years in various scrapes, about a dozen or so, and there were two Sons as well, who had tried to assassinate him way back when."

"All justifiable, in my opinion." Mom said and I was surprised. I wasn't expecting this bloodthirsty side to come from Mom, but I too agreed that it was justifiable.

"Yeah, I suppose they were justifiable, it wasn't like any of them were good people or innocents, but still, that kind of stuff sticks in your head for a long time." He said. Natasha nodded.

"I killed my father." She said and I was surprised to hear her say it. I didn't think she would want to mention that kind of thing, but looking at who all was there, it didn't really surprise me.

"Well, I never killed anyone, but I would if I had to." Dad said. "I think it's nuts how we don't execute criminals anymore in Canada or how they give those assholes on death row in the U.S.A. such compassion. Where was their compassion when they killed their victims? They just had something in the news about one of those jerks trying to say how killing him was inhumane treatment, yet he murdered a bunch of kids."

"Did they kill him?" Mom asked and Dad nodded. I felt good.

"Well, then they did the right thing. The dictatorships have the right idea. They don't dick around. Just bang, bang, bang, end of the problem and then donate the organs." Dad said.

"The Wara tends to make you learn stuff if they put you in jail," Rob said and I stared at him.

"The Wara put people in jail? Human jails?" I asked him and he shook his head.

"No, not human jails, but they do have places, secret buildings out in their territories that they can imprison people in. I heard this one story about a guy they found illegally trophy hunting on their land. They drug him back and put him in one of their jails. He was there for ten years, alone, except for a few rats. Every week, this alpha Wara guard would go in and beat the piss out of him. Then, one day, when the Wara was in there beating him, a rat came out and the Wara went to kill it. The guy jumped in front of it to defend it, offering up his life for the rat, and the Wara decided to let him go." He said to us. I was in awe.

"So what happened to him? Did he go back to his family and say a werewolf had him captive for all that time?" I asked him and he laughed.

"No, actually something really funny happened. He wound up marrying the Wara, the one that beat him up every day. He's a member of the Dragon Heads now."

The others laughed, but I looked at him. "The Dragon Heads?" I asked curiously, not hearing the term before and he looked at me and nodded.

"They are the elite members of the Grand Alliance. We try to have a few of every race there. Alpha's, Son's, Humans, and a few other secret ones as well." He said with a wink.

The conversation drifted then, and after a few more minutes of chatter, Rob excused himself and went home. Mom and Dad went to bed and Natasha and I decided to do the same. We had pulled a cot out of storage and put it in my room for her. It was a lot of fun sharing a room with her. As Natasha and I decided to get ready for bed, she brushed her teeth and got dressed in her pajamas, she looked at me and grinned.

"He's so hot! Is he single?" she asked me and I gasped. I never once thought of Rob that way before, or heard of anyone else who did.

"Him?" I asked her and she laughed. I was still dumbstruck. "Yeah, he's single, I guess... why? You're not interested in *him*, are you?" I asked her incredulously. She nodded with her eyes wide.

"Of course I am! He is very cute! And he seems really nice! And he's got a GREAT ass!" she replied and I thought I was going to gag.

"God! Gross!" I said to her and she just laughed.

"Well, he does! He's in good shape and he's funny and nice, and I bet you he would treat a woman pretty special. I'm surprised you haven't done anything with him."

"UGH! No way! I've known him all my life! He's like... I dunno... my Dad or something." I said to her, really freaked out at what she was saying.

"He's not that old. Your Dad is what, forty-five? Rob is ten years younger. I think he'd be really good in bed!" She said, and I knew she was now just teasing, trying to freak me out. It was kind of working.

"He's thirty-five. I think he's real nice and everything, he's a nice guy, but..." I said, not really sure how to put it all in words. I just wasn't attracted to him. Maybe it was because of Lord DeRom... I didn't know for sure.

"Well, I think he's a catch." She said matter-of-factly. "And I plan to get to know him a lot better."

As she went to sleep, I laid in my bed listening to her breathing as my mind started to race. I felt something I never felt before regarding Rob. Jealousy.

****

The next day I awoke to find Natasha gone already. When I went downstairs, I discovered that she had gone over to Rob's place. "She sure doesn't waste time," I said to myself as I ate my breakfast somewhat angrily.

I was halfway through when Mom came in. "Good morning! Your friend went over to Rob's. I think she has a crush on him." She said with a grin. It wasn't returned.

"Yeah, a bit sudden, don't you think? She just met him last night and she's already going to his house uninvited to throw herself at him." I said and Mom looked at me with surprise.

"Well, I don't see it as a bad thing. You aren't interested in him, I figured you would like the thought of your friend liking him," she said.

"She can like who she pleases, I just think it's too soon to be flirting with him, is all," I said, finishing my cereal.

"Oh, I wouldn't say she's jumping into bed with him or anything just yet, she just went to go talk to him. Pretty innocent, really. He's going to get her paperwork moved through to get her accepted as a Canadian faster. He has some connections in the government to help speed stuff like this along." Mom said, smirking at me.

"So she's using him to get citizenship." I shot back and Mom burst out laughing at me. I glared at her for a few seconds, wondering what was so funny about Natasha using Rob like that before I asked her, "What is so funny?"

"Oh, just you being jealous of Natasha. You had no interest in him what-so-ever all these years, and as soon as a girl shows interest in him, now you want him."

I gasped. "GROSS! I don't want HIM! He's like a family member or something!" I turned red.

"Right. Keep telling yourself that." Mom said, laughing

harder at me. It just made me madder and redder, but I don't think she gave a shit.

I went upstairs to change and get ready for the day. I went outside and was headed towards the barn when I saw his old truck pulling into the laneway, Natasha was in the passenger seat, all gaga over him.

"He's getting my citizenship papers processed really fast! Isn't that great news?" she bubbled happily as she got out of the truck.

"Wonderful." I shot back somewhat angrily as I walked past them and into the barn. I could feel their eyes on me, but I didn't turn or say a thing to them.

"Bitch! How dare she come here into my life and start taking over things! Waving her tits in everyone's faces, being a total skank!" I thought wildly to myself as I started cleaning up the barn, pitching hay wildly around with my pitchfork.

A few minutes later, I heard the truck start and Dad came into the barn and looked at me. He looked concerned and I stopped what I was doing, which basically was making a mess.

"Natasha is in the house, you should go say something to her. I think she thinks you're mad at her."

"I am mad at her." I shot back bluntly.

"What for?" he asked curiously.

"Being a tramp." I shot back.

"Being a tramp? With who?" he asked. I turned at him and looked at him like he was crazy.

"Who do you think?" I said at last.

"Rob? So what if she is, how does that bother you? She's your friend, he's your friend, you're not interested in him, and besides, they didn't do anything, she just went to talk to him about getting her citizenship quicker."

I ignored him for a bit, still flinging fresh straw around the barn floor.

"I think you're being childish, Jackette. Childish and selfish. You don't want him, but you don't want anyone else to have him, either. That man has been alone long enough, and he has suffered more loss than anyone his age ever should. If you *do* care for him you should want him to be happy. I think Natasha and him would make a fine couple." He said sternly and I stopped my straw flinging and turned to look at him. He was right.

I set the pitchfork down and felt tears running down my cheeks. "I know, Daddy... I'm sorry. I don't know what I was thinking."

He hugged me and I coughed from all the straw dust floating

around in the barn. He wiped my tears away and held me by the shoulders and looked me in the eye.

"Now, ask yourself this question. Do YOU want him?" he asked me and I shook my head no.

"Ok then, now ask yourself THIS question. Do you trust her?"

I thought for a second, then nodded my head hesitatingly.

"Don't you think you should give her a chance then? They are both alone in life, and it's not like there are many people around whom they can tell things. He's kinda limited to you or her, and you don't want him. Now I know for a fact he would love to be with you, but you don't want him... so doesn't he deserve to be with *someone* that will understand him and love him back?"

I nodded again, my eyes welling up with fresh tears.

"Ok then. Wipe your eyes, clean yourself off, and go in there and be happy for your friends," he said, giving me a smile and a hug before letting go.

I dusted myself off, wiped my face, and went into the house. I found Natasha sitting at the table with Mom, drinking coffee. Both of them turned to look at me, wondering what was going to happen.

I smiled and hugged Natasha and I could hear Mom sigh in relief. "Congratulations!" I said to Natasha, feeling bad for how I had acted earlier.

Dad came into the house and smiled at me. "So, did he say when you could expect to be a citizen?" He asked her and I released Natasha and sat in my usual place at the table.

"No, just that he had a contact in the government that would help move things along. He said something about having some sort of P, B, and B ceremony soon?" She said questioningly. Mom laughed and we all looked at her for an answer. "P, B, and B. Pizza, Burgers, and Beer." She said and we all chuckled. A part of me still was angry or jealous, I couldn't really tell which, but I subdued it.

"That's great news," I said to her and smiled at her again. "We should celebrate tonight!"

"Could we go to the movies? I've only ever gone to the movies twice in my life. I've always wanted to go see big Hollywood blockbuster." She said excitedly and I laughed.

"Twice in your life? Holy cow, we go twice a month as a rule." I said to her and she gasped. I looked at Mom and Dad and they both nodded. Dad then announced that he would see what was playing tonight, and then he pulled out his phone to find it online.

We ran upstairs and got ready. When we got downstairs, Mom and Dad were just finishing up with the animals out in the barn.

"Want to call him up, see if he feels like going out with us tonight?" Dad said, looking at me and motioning towards Rob's house with his head. I nodded. He smiled.

I got on the phone and rang his house. After three rings, he answered.

"City morgue, parts department," he said casually. He usually answered the phone with a smart assed comment like that. Sometimes, they were downright funny.

"Hey, how's it going?" I said. I was trying to sense something from him, interest or something. There was none.

"Good, how's things with you?" he asked in his usual tone. He was impossible to read.

"Good. Hey, we're all thinking on going to the movies tonight in Summerside to celebrate Natasha's joining us. Wanna come with us?" I asked him. After a few seconds of silence, he spoke.

"Tonight? Uhhh... maybe. What's playing?" he asked. I looked at Dad then and asked him what was playing.

"I was thinking we could go see that action movie that's out. What's his face is in it... the bald British guy... everything else playing looks lame. There are a few kid's shows and some sappy romance flicks... and some historical one about Queen Elizabeth isn't horrible looking." He told me. I relayed them to Rob.

He hemmed and hawed. "I'd rather go see the historical one, to be honest... but whatever you guys want to go see is fine with me. I'm easy to please." He said. A part of me wondered if he was, in fact, 'easy to please' and what it would be like to please him, but I kept it silent. These thoughts were driving me crazy.

"He said whatever we want to go see would be fine. What say we just go down there, get some dinner, and then see what we feel like afterwards?" I said to Dad and Mom and they shrugged and agreed.

I told the same to Rob and he agreed and said he'd be right over. By the time he showed up, Mom and Dad were both cleaned up and we were ready to go.

The trip to Summerside was about an hour, with one stop for gas and another for Natasha to get her picture taken by a big field of potatoes. We pulled into the town limits, drove by the theatre and checked out the movie times, then decided to go for pizza at a place not far from the theatre.

It was weird sitting there with all of them. I was the youngest, then Natasha, then Rob, then Mom and Dad, but the total of the attention was on Rob and Natasha. I couldn't tell if Rob was interested in her, or me, for that matter, he always seemed to be closed when it came to displaying his emotions... Especially love ones.

"So, any news?" Dad asked him and he looked up from his slice of all-meat pizza and shook his head. "No, pretty quiet, actually... which frightens me a bit. I hate it when things are quiet. Usually means they are up to something. I hear that the Sisters of Slaughter are still raining hell on the Taxiss nobles. Things are going well for them in their little civil war, but that's it. No real new stuff. Did he say anything last time you spoke to him, Jackette?" Rob asked as he looked at me.

I shook my head. "No. He never said anything new was going on, really. Why? You think we have a shit storm on the way?"

He just shrugged and resumed his eating. Not much stopped him from a slice of pizza. I think if the end of the world was coming you would either find him in a pizza place or a burger joint before you would find him anywhere else. He was definitely a fast food junkie.

"I hope nothing happens. I like just getting to learn things quietly and on my own time, not getting thrown into situations with no warning. I hope the Royal Alliance is better than the Grand Alliance when it comes to that." Natasha said, sipping on an orange soda pop. I had told her that Prince Edward Island had the best orange soda pop on earth, and after trying some, she was hooked. Their lime soda pop that they used to have was better, but only when it was in the old glass bottles. Once they had shifted everything over into cans and plastic bottles, it just wasn't the same.

"The Royal Alliance is nothing like the Grands," Rob said after he had swallowed. "We tend to fly by the seat of our pants more often than not."

"Small wonder why that is," Dad said laughing. "If we were kept in the loop a bit more, perhaps we'd be a little less sporadic and better with our assistance."

"True enough," Rob said, biting off another piece of pizza. He was on his fourth piece and showed little sign of slowing down. As he finished chewing, he spoke again. "You guys do realize the reason I don't keep you all in the loop as much as I would like. You're all only new and low-generation allies. You don't have the mental abilities to shield what you know from other people who can probe your thoughts. If I told you everything I could tell you, you'd have it in your head and the first skeeter that came by would learn everything you knew. You guys are too much of a security risk to tell the whole truth, too. We have to keep a lot of things to ourselves. Once you get to be seventh or eighth generation, give me a call and I'll fill you in on all the good stuff and gory details."

"What's a skeeter?" Dad asked him and Rob laughed. I knew what Rob was talking about, but nobody else seemed to know what it was.

"Slang for mosquito... bloodsucker... no offence to Natasha's heritage, but I'm not referring to vampires here, I'm referring to certain individuals that can probe the minds of others. Astral spies. They can suck the thoughts right out of your head... Like a mosquito sucking out blood..." he said and I nodded in agreement.

Natasha looked at him then. "So you are saying that there are people out there that can read other people's minds? Gain valuable information and stuff just by looking at them?"

"Yup." He said nonchalantly, reaching for his fifth slice. "I lost a lot of good friends and Allies that way. That's the problem with new allies wanting info. You just can't give it to them straight and true because everybody will know it the first time a skeeter comes around. A friend will only take being told bullshit for so long before they turn on you. The sad thing is it was all for their own protection. We'd love to have you know it all, it would make our lives a lot easier, but we can't because your minds are too readable. Low generational allies are like a clear pane of glass to an astral spy."

We let him eat in peace then, realizing we had stirred up old feelings for him. I'd ask Mom and Dad about it later on, as they seemed to know what he was talking about.

Dad looked at his watch and announced that it was almost

movie time. We got the rest of the pizza to go and went over to the theatre. Rob surprised us by buying the tickets for everybody.

We sat together, with Mom and Dad side by side, Dad at the aisle, Mom next in, then Rob, then me, and then Natasha furthest in. Natasha got more than her share of stares from the guys while we were in getting our tickets... and even a lot of stares from the girls. A few probably even wondered if they should ask for her autograph, thinking she was some movie starlet or something.

I couldn't tell you what the movie was about. I lost interest in it after the first ten minutes when I noticed that Jesse was sitting a few rows ahead of us and off to the side. He had come in late once the theatre had darkened, so he had not noticed us sitting there. I leaned over to point him out to Natasha.

"So that's him." She said and I nodded. "Do you want me to go down there and kick him in the testicles for you?" She asked and I laughed. It would be funny to see Jesse getting the crap knocked out of him by her, but it would only cause trouble and ruin the night for everyone. I wanted revenge on him, though, that much was for certain. I just had to play my cards straight to make sure I got it.

I fumed through the whole movie, staring at him. The girl was just another innocent victim, I was sure, another girl he'd get pregnant and then dump flat. I'm sure it bugged him to see me not walking around with a puffed-up belly. I found out afterwards that he had told his friends one day that he wanted to have twelve kids… One for every beer in a case. He was likely well on the way to that.

The movie ended at last and we got up to leave. Jesse and his date managed to get out before I could go up to them and ruin their night, and I was pretty sure he hadn't even seen us. I kinda wished he did.

I went to the bathroom after the movie ended and Natasha came in with me, cursing the giant-sized sodas they sell and the movies. "I had to pee for the last hour! I wish they would bring back intermissions! When did they stop those?" She said from the next stall, her thick accent sounding hilarious saying stuff like that.

She got out of her stall and looked at me. "So that was the man that used you, that's Jesse. Was that girl he was with his girlfriend or is she another girl he's got on some strings?"

"Another girl on the string." I corrected her as I balled up a wad of used paper towel that I had dried my hands off with and tossed at the waste bin. I missed, cursing.

"We need to give him a taste of his own drugs." She said and I chuckled at her. "Medicine. A taste of his own medicine, and yes, I'd love to get revenge on him. Any ideas?" I asked her and she shook her head, thinking.

"We could ask Rob or Lord DeRom to help?" she said and I

shook my head.

"I don't want to get them involved in my troubles. I got myself into this mess, I don't want to need them to get my revenge for me, too... but it would be funny to hear what he'd do."

"Revenge for a Son tends to be a bloody, pain-filled affair." She said seriously, her voice low. "I heard once that they skinned a man alive, and then kept him alive. They tanned his skin and put it up on display. That man is still alive, and he looks hideous."

"God!" I gasped. "That's disgusting! What did the guy do to get them so mad?" I asked her and she just shrugged.

"I'm not sure, but I saw this man with my own eyes. It served to be a good reminder not to get them angry. Have you ever heard of a man named Franklin El Zia? He was one of their contacts in the Middle East. Anyhow, he had become a Moslem, but he was also a high-ranking member of the Grand Alliance long before he converted to Islam. He took a girl, had sex with her, and she was his servant girl, but to the Son, they seen it as she was unwilling... and too young... so they took out his man parts, then his eyes, then switched their places, and then, at last, tore his head off and gave it to the girl. Apparently, it is the standard punishment for rape. The Sons don't rape, and the females are equal with the males, usually priestesses, so to hurt a female sexually to them is a very bad thing. It was female Sons that did this to him."

"Well, I sort of agree with them on that," I said to her softly as we left the bathroom to find everyone else. They were in the lobby, waiting for us.

We had to stop at a burger place for Rob before we left Summerside for the drive west. Three burgers; two more for him and one for his elderly dog Moon. He spoiled that dog rotten.

On the drive home, after he had finished one of the burgers, I looked at him. He looked so normal just sitting there, I had a hard time believing he wasn't human, well, not fully human, at least. He looked peaceful, happy, just sitting there chatting to us like he was just another human out for a night at the movies. Anyone looking at him would never dream he was anything other than what he appeared to be, just an average guy. I guess that's what made the Sons so damn spooky. They could be anyone.

Natasha was laughing about something Dad said and Mom was laughing at Natasha's laugh when Rob looked at me and caught me staring at him. He just winked at me and I turned my head and stared out the window. Did he think I liked him? I didn't, did I? I was just curious about him. What was he thinking? God only knew. Man or werewolf, whatever he was, he was a good person. I just didn't know if he really wanted me or if I really wanted him. But either way, I still didn't feel overly great having Natasha chase him.

Chapter Six

Moonshine and Memories

The next morning, I woke up and found Natasha gone again. I cursed and then dove out of bed and into the shower. I was out the door and on my way to his house before Mom could even say good morning to me.

Nobody was in his house, but his truck was home. I walked around his yard until I seen Moon walking around the backyard untied and I knew he had to be around somewhere. Moon was always either with him or tied. I patted her and she dropped and rolled over so I could rub her silver-furred belly. She was a sweet old dog, overfed and spoiled rotten, but a total sweetheart. He babied her more than most people baby their children. She was professionally groomed regularly, was fed nothing but the best, and now she was wearing some type of new collar with a pretty gemstone on it. She had several. The dog had more jewelry than I did.

I heard a radio playing in the shed and I walked towards it. I could hear voices coming from it, but I noticed that the windows were all taped over with cardboard. He and Natasha were in there together, hiding from me, I bet, probably doing it.

The door opened and Rob and Dad walked out. Dad looked

at me with a surprised look on his face. "What are you doing here?" he asked me calmly and I couldn't say anything. I was just frozen there on the ground in front of his shed feeling stupid.

"Don't go in there, Jackette. You won't like what you smell. That stuff sticks on your clothes for a long, long time. Trust me." Dad said to me then went to the house, leaving me sitting on his lawn. I looked at Rob, who came out holding a quart bottle and staring at the sun through it.

"Wanna drink? This is some of the best moonshine your Dad and me have ever made!" he said with a grin, offering me the bottle. I just shook my head and left then, going back home. I felt like a total idiot.

I went home and helped Mom clean the house, which was only fair since I had messed up most of it. Mom told me that Natasha had woken up early and went to Charlottetown to fill out immigration papers. Things were moving quickly in that department. She would be a Canadian in a few more days, thanks to Rob's connections.

Around six o'clock, she showed up, carrying bags of Chinese food. We were lucky she did because Mom, Dad, and I were busy in the barn and had lost track of time. Suppertime had almost come and gone. We usually ate early.

We ate a huge oriental feast of fried rice, General Tao's

chicken, moo goo guy pan, chicken balls, and beef and broccoli. When we were all stuffed to the ears, Mom put the leftovers in the fridge.

A few days later, Rob showed up, not coming inside but stayed out in the barn talking to Dad. When he left, Dad came into the house smiling drunkenly, reeking of the moonshine they had made.

Rob called once to cancel our Wednesday night talk and it was almost another week before we seen him again. As it was, it was us who went down to see him. We were kinda getting worried about him.

We found him drunk as a skunk, sitting in a lawn chair out back of his house. Moon was laying on the ground next to him, sleeping.

"Howdy folks!" he said as we walked around the end of the house and found him there. An empty mason jar was sitting nearby.

"Haven't seen you in a while, we were getting worried. Normally, you're around more often." Dad said to him. Rob didn't go on benders very often, I had only seen him truly drunk a handful of times, to be honest, but when he did tie one on, there usually was a reason for it.

Rob nodded. "Yeah... I was busy, though... in my head, and

then out there... and then here..." he said slurring, motioning at first to the shed and then to the bottle.

"Good God man, you've been drinking this stuff all week," Dad said to him, then looked around the corner of the house. "Holy shit, yeah, you have... let's see, there's one two three four five six... Jesus man, you drank six jars of this shit? Are you trying to kill yourself? And Lord DeRom? You know that you're kind shouldn't drink to excess! Remember your uncle?" Dad said to him angrily as he counted up the empties that were sitting around the corner of the house.

Rob just nodded. "Yeah, yeah, I know I know... don't worry, he's good and dormant. I wasn't trying to hurt him or nothing. I was... I'm just having a hard time lately, is all." He said with a grin, but it was a bad attempt to cover up the fact that he was very near tears.

Dad looked at Mom for more info. She knew his past better than anyone else. He had grown up around her and she had even babysat him a few times. She frowned for a second, thinking, then grimaced.

I went over to her to find out the details while Dad spoke to him. "Fifteenth anniversary of C.K.'s death. Shit, I should have remembered. I totally forgot." She said to me. I didn't know C.K. He was gone before I was able to remember. It was weird, he had lived here since before I was born, had always been around, and had told me things no one else knew, yet I still knew nothing about his history, his friends, or his family.

I went back to talk to him while Mom explained things to Dad. A few seconds later, they both returned. "Everything... ok... in there?" Mom asked him, motioning towards the house. Rob looked at her and nodded. "Oh yeah baby, It's O.K. Work first, then play. I know... I know. Nothing lying around you guys shouldn't see. I have all the special stuff tucked away from prying eyes."

He often had Son tech or other stuff around he didn't let us know about. Usually, he had it in the back room, but once in a while, especially if he was on a bender, it'd be just lying around where he left it last. He'd often be studying something when no one was around, documenting histories of various items, or finding out what they did, if anything. He didn't like having us see them.

"Let's get you inside, get you cleaned up. Jesus man, did you piss yourself or something? You're damp feeling." Dad said as he grabbed him and began to help him to his feet.

"Huh?" Rob said and then shook his head. "No, no, it rained last night." He said. Dad gasped slightly and then laughed at him.

"You slept on the lawn chair last night? In the rain?" He asked. He just nodded his head.

"Sleep? I never slept a wink last night... night before either, or the one before that one. Just got to drinking after I talked to you that day, came here, and been here ever since. Went in the house a few times a day to check on things, feed Moon and stuff... took her out here to play in the sun this morning after the ground dried up." He said, pointing at the dog. Dad had him almost to his feet and his sudden turn in direction towards Moon sent them both off balance. They toppled over the lawn chair and went headlong into the grass.

He laughed, lying on the ground in a soggy heap with Dad, all tangled up with each other and the old reclining lawn chair, face down in the grass. Mom, Natasha, and I went over to help them up. Dad was not amused but said nothing, while Rob had a bloody lip and was laughing to kill himself.

"Oopsy! Sorry Steve." He said between fits of drunken laughter. "You O.K., dude?"

"I'm fine, just get off me, will ya? You weigh a ton." Dad said coolly from underneath him. Dad had taken the brunt of the fall.

Rob got to his feet with a lot of help from us and he put an arm over Mom's shoulder. "Thanks baby!" he said cheerfully and Mom just nodded.

"Stop calling me baby, will you?" she said with a chuckle and he just laughed.

"Nobody puts baby in the corner!" he hooted and then stumbled towards the house. Natasha helped Dad up, while I helped Mom take Rob inside his house.

The house was clean... very, very clean. "Come on, I'll help you get to bed," Dad said as he came in behind us. He replaced me at his side and he and Mom took him upstairs to his room to sleep it off.

"Does he do this often?" Natasha asked me as they disappeared around the corner at the head of the stairs.

"No," I replied. "Only when he's nervous or remembering bad stuff. I've never seen him this drunk before in my life, though. He usually goes on a good bender once in a while, usually around Christmas and in the summer sometimes, but not to this degree. Fifteenth anniversary of his best friend's death, Mom says. He must be taking it hard this year." I told her and she nodded. We looked around his home, walking around the downstairs kitchen and living room, the room he had as a library and the old parlor. The house was well over a hundred years old, but he kept it meticulously maintained. It was a very beautiful old home.

"I love the clock," I told Natasha as I showed her a huge grandfather clock that ticked away deeply in the back of the parlor. "It's old... as old as the house." I said to her and she admired it.

"Impressive." She said and stroked the side of it. It was so highly polished that it almost felt wet to the touch.

A large screen TV sat in the living room on a beautiful handmade wooden stand that matched exactly the hardwood floor and window frames. A black leather chair and couch, a wooden coffee table and end tables all perfectly matched the flooring and trim as well. On the walls hung several large Robert Bateman prints of various nature scenes and odd pictures of Rob and other people throughout the years. I thought it was funny to see them really. They had been here for years and I had been in this house dozens, if not hundreds, of times, but this was the first time that I really noticed them.

We sat on the couch and I noticed a large, leather-bound book on the coffee table. I opened it up and realized it was a photo album. Natasha and I leafed through it, looking at dozens of old photos, many of them black and white.

I recognized the house in them and realized that they were old family photos of his grandfather, father, aunts and uncles. There were also clippings of obituaries from the newspapers of family members, and as we were leafing through I noticed one of a young man that stood out.

"Who's he?" Natasha said, trying to read the small print. It was dark in the living room, even with the lights on. He kept the window blinds drawn most of the way down to avoid glare on the television and the walls were painted dark, pool table felt green, so it tended to mute light. There were no ceiling-mounted lights, but he did have several lamps. I flicked on one of the nearby ones so we could see it better.

"That's him," I said to Natasha. "He was his best friend. He died fifteen years ago now. He was an Ally, too. He was one of their priests. Mom and Dad's good friend, too."

"He was a priest?" Natasha said of the man in the photo. He didn't look to be very old. "He's quite good-looking. Too good-looking to be a priest." She said and I chuckled. He was a young, good looking guy, and 'priest' wasn't the thing that popped into mind when you saw him.

"Yeah. He overdosed, they say. I guess he suffered from depression really bad. Being in the Alliance wouldn't likely help that much, either. Rob took it really hard. It's understandable. It was his best friend, after all."

"Sad," Natasha said, then looked up. Mom and Dad were coming down the stairs.

"Is he asleep?" I asked them and they nodded. "Yeah, he is... finally, we should maybe stay here until he wakes up... I don't like leaving anyone that drunk alone." Mom said and Dad nodded.

"I'll go home and make sure the animals are all ok. You girls want to come back with me to pack some things?" He asked and we both nodded and got up. Mom seen the photo album and came up to us.

"What's that?" she asked and I showed her. She seen the photo and nodded. "C.K. What a shame that was." She said. Dad looked into the room and nodded.

"Yeah, that was a rough time for everyone. C.K. had a drug problem before he became an Ally, but he had gotten clean. He was doing really good for himself, but not good enough in his eyes. He was always worried about the "Big Picture". Then the stress and the depression set in a few years later, and I guess he struggled with it for a time and it eventually won out. Really sad time for all of us." He said. "Ok you guys, let's go. Honey, you gonna stay here or do you want to come with us?"

"I'll stay here in case he wakes up." Mom said. "Just bring me a change of clothes and my bathroom stuff."

"Ok, will do," Dad said and we left.

When we were driving back, Natasha looked at Dad and asked him if Rob and Mom ever had a thing. When he asked why she thought that, she said because he kept calling her 'baby'. Dad laughed and shook his head.

"No, they are just old friends. I guess you've never seen

"Dirty Dancing." Eliza and Rob were good friends before I met either of them. Apparently, one time, she was staining the floor and trapped herself in a corner and he came and found her. He's been calling her "Baby" ever since. I guess you'd have to see the movie to get the joke."

We drove into our laneway and Dad went to the barn to look after the animals. Natasha and I went upstairs to pack our stuff. I packed Mom's bag as well, and Dad's, and had everything in the car waiting for him when he was finished out at the barn.

We drove back to the Host's house and found Mom sitting at the kitchen table, flipping through the same old photo album Natasha and I had been looking at.

"Good Lord, there's a lot of history here. Some of these pictures are over a century old." She said. Dad nodded his head. "Yeah, he is a clinger to the past I'll give him that. He loves his history. Too damn much so, at times. He's got to learn to let a lot of this shit go."

I went to work in the kitchen, looking through his cupboards for something to make us eat. He had lots of meat in his freezer, every kind of steak and cut you could imagine for the most part. Every year he bought a whole beef from us, as well as half a pork, and at least a dozen chickens. We usually raised a few animals every year for sale but our farming was mostly potatoes. Most farmers in our area were potato farmers, the Island being a major producer of potatoes for the world, but a lot of the smaller, local farmers like us had a few cows, pigs, and chickens for sale in the fall to sell to the locals. It paid to diversify.

I fished out a package of steaks and put them on the grill. We ate and then made sure that Moon was fed and looked after as well. After that was done, Dad went out to the shed to make sure things were O.K. out there and came in a while later. "Well, I can tell you this, he's out of shine. Must have drank two gallons of the stuff. I'm amazed he has a liver left in him. Double run stuff, too. Potent."

We spent the evening watching "Dirty Dancing" and eating popcorn on his couch. We made up beds where we could, with Mom and Dad sleeping in his spare room. Natasha and I slept in the living room on an inflatable mattress. It was strange sleeping in his house. I had only ever done it once before, when I was small when Dad and Mom were remodeling our house. The big clock ticking rhythmically put me right to sleep.

I awoke the next morning to the smell of bacon and fresh coffee. I got up and went into the kitchen and found Rob in there cooking breakfast. He had pancakes, toast, hash browns, and a mountain of bacon cooked up for us. He seemed chipper and none the worse for wear, except his voice was hoarse and he had bags under his eyes. "Hey there, hope you guys are hungry. I made a shitload of breakfast for ya's." He said cheerfully. "Thanks for... well... everything..." he said and I nodded. "That's what we're for," I said, giving him a hug. It felt strangely good to hug him.

I wanted him and me to be like we were again, not with all this weird sexual tension and shit. He hugged me back tight, and I returned it. He smelled good, like clean laundry and freshly ironed sheets. A bit of cologne wafted up from him as well, which only made him smell better. He must have gotten up and showered before coming down here. I was surprised I never heard the shower going. I must have been out like a light.

We released each other and our eyes met. His were a piercing blue, dark and deep, and so very full of emotion that it surprised me. They stared into mine, searing right down into my soul, it seemed, like they were lasers shooting out into the vastness of space. I immediately realized that Natasha was right about him being handsome. Quite handsome, in fact. I wondered why I hadn't noticed it before. I felt myself leaning closer towards him, craving his lips against mine. The sound of a toilet flushing broke the spell and I backed away from him just in time to avoid having Dad see us. I blushed, even though I had no reason to.

"Good morning! How's the head?" he asked him and Rob just nodded and smiled weakly. "It's a big on the achy side this morning. Thanks for looking after me yesterday, Steve... I was in pretty rough shape." "You O.K. now? I'm not going to find you passed out in that lawn chair again, am I? Getting on into fall, you know... not overly good sleeping outdoors weather." Dad said to him and then laughed. I laughed, too. Rob only nodded his head like he was being scolded, which only made us laugh harder. He was laughing too, at the end of it. "Yeah, yeah, I'll be good. Now shut up and eat something. I made a ton of chow. Hope you guys are hungry."

We ate the breakfast after we woke everyone up. Mom had left early to go check the farm, so it was just Dad, Natasha, Rob and I. We ate our fill and still had a bunch left. He fed a lot of the leftovers to Moon, then tossed the rest in the fridge.

"Well ladies, Steve, I thank you once again for drunk-sitting me. I'm off to Charlottetown now. Would either of you lovely young ladies care to come along for a drive? I'm just going for a quick trip up to get a few things and I'm coming right back. Might cruise around for a bit to sightsee. I'd ask you to come along as well Steve, but frankly, well, you're a guy. And you're ugly." He said with a grin. Natasha and I both burst out laughing.

"Asshole," Dad said with a laugh. "Fine, fuck you all then. I have stuff to do at home anyways."

Rob was laughing hard then, as were Natasha and I. "Come on then, let's go. You want a lift home there, ugly? Looks like Baby stole your car." He said to Dad as we walked outside.

"Yeah sure, Mr. Smart Ass." He said and then hopped in the back of the truck. Rob got in the driver's side and I leapt for the middle, making Natasha sit on the passenger side between us. I planned to stay there for the day too.

Chapter Seven
Revenge

I'm not sure what all he had to do in Charlottetown, but he didn't spend much time there like he said. He went to a few of the big government buildings, then a few farm supply stores for a few minutes, then we were on our way again. You could see his shoulders releasing tension the further west we drove into the country and away from town. He didn't like all the hustle and bustle. Too many people for his liking.

He took us out to eat while we were there an Italian place not far from the waterfront. It was nice and would have been romantic if it was just two people. I wasn't sure which one of us he was trying to romance, if he was trying to romance either of us, but I found myself jealous of Natasha once again.

Of course, I felt like the wilting daisy next to a rose going anywhere with her. Every place we went, there were people downright gawking at her. She was utterly beautiful, I had to admit that... and I considered her my best friend. I just wasn't sure if I should have told Dad that I wasn't interested in Rob that day in the barn because all of a sudden, I sure was regretting saying that.

We were just outside of Summerside when he asked us if we needed anything while we were there. I said no, as did Natasha, but he stopped at the mall for dog food, so we went in with him to look around.

We were in there about five minutes when I spied Jesse chatting to a girl at the jewelry counter. The girl was totally enthralled with whatever bull shit he was shoveling her way.

Natasha looked at me, then at Jesse. "Isn't that the man that got you pregnant?" she asked me softly as we watched him from around a clothing rack. I nodded.

"Yeah, that's him," I said to her. "Look at him, God, he's such an asshole! I just want to go over there and kick him right in the nuts!"

Natasha laughed, then looked at me. "I'll get him going good. Watch this!" she told me. I had no idea what she was doing, but if nothing else, it would probably save the poor clerk at the counter from him... and get him all sexually frustrated.

I stayed at my post and watched as Natasha grabbed a nearby empty cart and threw in a bunch of lingerie, then walked over to the counter where he was. As soon as Jesse seen her, he actually jolted from shock.

She was slightly off to the side, looking at some earrings, when he approached her. He just left the girl at the counter hanging. I could tell that she was pissed off at having been thrown away so obviously.

He said something to Natasha and she looked up at him and smiled. I couldn't hear what they were saying since they were too far away, but whatever it was, he was pouring it on thick and she was acting all flattered and interested.

I saw him give her something and then she left. A few minutes later she returned from behind me, having skirted around numerous racks to not let anyone see her.

"He gave me his phone number." She said with a laugh. "What were you thinking letting that pig have sex with you? He's an imbecile. *And* he's disgusting." She said. I just shook my head in frustration.

"I have no idea. So, now that we have his number, we're going to have to call him. You never gave him *our* number, did you?" I asked her. She shook her head.

"No, I tell him I just moved to Canada and I have not gotten a telephone yet, but I tell him I will call him soon. He seen this stuff in my cart and his eyes went big." She said, laughing. "He now is... how you say... *very* horny for me."

We laughed and then made our way back to the truck. Rob was out there already, waiting for us.

"What's so funny?" he asked us and we shook our heads.

"Nothing, just Natasha met Jesse. He's all gaga over her now." I said to him, he frowned.

"Don't tell me you're going to go out with him too?" he said incredulously.

She looked at him and made a face then shook her head. "Good heavens, no!" she said, laughing. "I just want to torment him."

"Ah. Hell hath no fury like a woman scorned." He said. I chuckled and nodded, but Natasha seemed perplexed. She apparently had no idea where the quote had come from. Most thought it was a Shakespearean quote, but it was actually from a play called "The Mourning Bride" written by a guy called William Congreve back in 1697. Thank God for drama class back in High School.

"It means that there is nothing worse than a pissed-off woman," I said to Natasha and she grinned and nodded in understanding and agreement. She was perfect for getting my revenge on Jesse. She was everything he could ever hope for, and she was my best friend... and if she was out with Jesse tormenting him, she couldn't be chasing after Rob.

****

She waited three days to call Jesse, and then she used a payphone... in Summerside. "Hello? Is this Jesse?" she asked him. He seemed confused for a second until he figured out who was calling him, then he was extremely alert and happy.

"Hey there gorgeous! How's it going?" he said to her. I was listening in, and I rolled my eyes. He used to say the exact same thing to me all the time. God, I hated him.

"I'm well, and yourself?" she asked him, her voice just oozing sex over the phone lines. The scary thing was, it wasn't really any different than how she normally spoke.

"I'm good baby. I was just thinking of you... wishing you'd call me." He said. I rolled my eyes again.

"Well, I make your wish come true, it seems." She said. I giggled evilly, trying to be silent. I didn't know what she was up to, but it would undoubtedly be nasty. She had a real nasty sense of humor in her. I loved it.

They spoke for a bit, just stupid stuff mostly, before Jesse asked her if she'd like to go for a drive, maybe a walk on the beach. She looked at me and shrugged, then said yes. "Great," Jesse said to her. "I'll pick you up. I drive a blue Cutlass Supreme. Where are you at?"

She looked at me with a panicked look. I told her to tell him to pick her up at the coffee shop on Water Street. We were near there already. She told him the address and then hung up. She then started to ask me questions about him, where he would take her, what she should do, etc. She even asked about sex, was he any good, how big he was, and even if he was circumcised. He wasn't either, I told her, but I wondered why it would matter. She wouldn't tell me why.

Less than an hour later, he showed up. I sat in the car across the street in a parking lot, watching carefully. She went out to his car and got in. I pulled out and followed, trying to be discrete.

They drove around Summerside for a bit and then went to the most expensive restaurant in town. I had told Natasha to make him pay for being a jerk and apparently, she was taking it literally. They were in there almost an hour before leaving.

I followed them for a bit and as soon as he went down towards Chelton beach, I knew exactly where he was taking her, to the same place on the beach that he had taken me.

They were there for a while, almost three hours to be exact, before leaving. I didn't see them leave the car, but I didn't know if they had gone to the back seat or not. She told me she wouldn't sleep with him, but I didn't know if I trusted her or not. Or if I trusted him not to use booze or drugs on her to get what he wanted.

He dropped her back off at the coffee shop, and I waited for a few minutes out in the parking lot until he left before going in to meet her. She was laughing when I got there.

"Oh my dear Jackette, I really need to teach you how to tell good men from bad men. He is... how you say it... idiot! He is also idiot who is going to go home to have very cold shower."

I laughed at that. So she didn't have sex with him. Good. That would just stroke Jesse's ego and he deserved nothing of the sort.

"I tell him big pile of bull poops. I say that I moved here and am divorced and that I am very lonely but very religious. He very much tried to have sex with me. He used horrible lines on me, tried to give me alcohol and marijuana, but I told him, no, I am a very religious woman. I tell him I cannot have sex with a man unless I am married to him, but also that I am very lonely... and want sex very much. So say to him, well, Ok, we can have sex. Let me see it. So he pulls out his penis and I look at it and say, OH No! I Cannot! I want to so bad, but you are not circumcised! I cannot have sex with a man who is not circumcised. Then I ask him to take me back here."

I was laughing hard then. "So he left feeling all horny, and he'll try to get in your pants again, but you'll just keep saying no?" I asked her and she shrugged and then nodded.

"I could bankrupt him if we go out again. Dinner was over two hundred dollars, and he's going to take me to a play at the theatre downtown and the tickets are a hundred dollars each." She said and I gasped and then laughed harder.

"Then I will get him to buy me things at the stores... I will make him suffer, do not worry." She said with a grin and I took into more laughter.

We drove back home, talking about what we were going to put Jesse through when she got quiet and looked at me. "Do you love Rob?" she asked me and I paused.

"No, not romantically... of course not. He's like my father or something." I said to her, lying. I used to think that way of him until the other day when she said she was interested in him. Now, I couldn't get him out of my mind.

"I think you are lying to me." She said and smiled. "I see how you look at him when I am around. You don't want me and him together."

I was quiet for a bit. She was right, but I wasn't sure if I really wanted him or not. If she backed off and said she wasn't interested in him, I wondered if I really would be interested in him.

"I don't know," I said to her softly. "He's been around since I was born, he's a lot older than me... by almost fifteen years... and I think he likes me too... I just don't know if I like him for the right reasons or, if I like him at all, or if I like him because you like him and I'm scared that if you and him get together, then I will lose him. He is very dear to me, I'm just not sure in what way."

Natasha was quiet after I said all that. I felt bad, but it was everything I was feeling and now it was all out in the open. She looked at me after a bit and smiled.

"Well, I will stay away from him *that* way then. I won't date him unless you are sure you do not love him." She said. "You are my best friend, Jackette. I do not want to let a man come between us. He is yours if you want him. But if you do not want him, I think I would like to date him... if he'd have me."

I looked at her then and nodded. "Thank you, Natasha. I appreciate that. I don't know what my heart wants most of the time. I thought I wanted Jesse, and I thought he wanted me, but look at how that turned out. I just don't know what's best for me. I doubt I ever will. It seems that whatever I should have, I don't want and whatever I shouldn't have, I want. I'm all messed up, I'm built backwards or something."

Natasha laughed. "That's called being a woman. It's our prerogative to be indecisive and to change our minds. It's just how we are."

I smiled. "Yeah, you're right there. I just wish that for once I knew my own heart."

"You'll know it when it speaks to you. I think if when you kiss a man and your heart does that little jump inside, you will know. If it's just O.K. but nothing special, then it isn't really love, you know?" Natasha said.

I nodded in agreement. I just wasn't sure if I actually wanted to be with Rob or not. I mean, I would always be his Ally, and I'd hopefully always be his Aide, I just wasn't sure that if we did start dating, I'd always be his lover. It'd be super awkward to be his lover and then break up, but still have to see each other all the time.

We arrived home and found Mom and Dad still up, which was strange because it was late when we got home. I looked at them and they came over to me and hugged me. Something was wrong, seriously wrong.

"He's missing." They said and I knew they were talking about Rob. "The house looks like a tornado went through it, there's blood all over the place, windows are smashed, and we found this in the backyard," Dad said as he threw something on the counter. It was an ornamental dagger of vampire design. Taxiss design, to be precise.

Chapter Eight
Death

We went to his house and found poor Moon, who was terrified and hiding under the porch. We had to drag her out by her collar and we decided to take her home with us. I was scared. There was blood all over the house, and whatever had happened had not gone down easy. We started cleaning and were putting plastic over the broken windows when a car drove into the laneway and two very large men came to the door.

"Who are you?" One of them asked us calmly. I wasn't sure if they were police or not, but somehow I doubted it. Police didn't tend to look that way.

Dad looked at them and decided to use code. "We're just a friend of a friend. We live down the road. Eliza and Steve MacNeill, this is our daughter Jackette and that's her friend Natasha." The man looked at the other man, who just nodded. "Friend of a friend" was code for Ally.

"You're his Allies then?" They asked, but it wasn't so much a question as a statement. Dad nodded, unsure as to what was going to happen then.

"Excellent. I am Karl Gustav and this is Mike Sadum, the Son Council sent us. We have reason to believe that the Host of

Emperor DeRom has been abducted by the lower-end members of the Taxiss vampire Clan."

****

"Why would vampires kidnap him?" I said to Natasha as I sobbed into my pillow. Four days had passed since he had gone missing. I recognized the dagger as the same one the members of Falcon's gang wore. Taxiss Clan daggers. Mike and Karl had verified it as well.

"I don't know," Natasha said sadly. "It is foolish of them to do it. The Son's will wipe them out."

"Oh God, I hope they don't kill him... I don't know what I'll do if they kill him..." I said, breaking out into fresh sobs. Natasha came over to the bed and hugged me. She was crying too.

The phone rang and a few minutes later, I heard Mom yelling for us to come downstairs. We got down there and she was sitting at the table, her eyes wet and red.

"That was Karl and Mike. They found him. They think..." She said and then broke down crying. I ran over to her and hugged her and bawled my eyes out as well. Natasha broke out into fresh tears as well and then ran outside. A few minutes later, she came back with Dad, who came into the house in a panic and looked at us, then turned away and faced the corner angrily, he slammed his fist into the wall several times, then put his head in his arms on the counter. He was there a few minutes, then stood up and turned around to look at Mom.

"What did they say?" he asked her and she sniffed back tears and began.

"Mike and Karl, they found Lord DeRom's body in the woods out back of the house. They think he was stabbed to death, but it was hard to tell from the amount of... damage... that was done to the body."

"I'm going over there." He said firmly, got up and headed out the door. Natasha and I went with him. Mom stayed home, simply unable to see his body.

We tore out the laneway and went to his house as fast as we could. Mike and Karl were both waiting for us.

Karl spoke. "We found a body, a Son body, white, out that way just in the woods." He said dully. Both he and Mike looked exhausted and somber.

"Can I go see him?" I asked and they looked at me and shook their heads. "You don't want to see that. There's not much left of him. He was torn up pretty bad. They severely mutilated the body...

and then animals found it."

Natasha and I both burst into tears once again and Dad just trembled and nodded. "I want to go see him." He said at last and Mike and Karl gave up trying to convince him otherwise and only nodded.

They took us to where he lay. It wasn't far from where I had hidden that first night I had seen Son's for the first time, all liquored up on gin and covered in No-Scent. There were a lot of broken branches around and torn-up ground, and over by a tree, there was a blue plastic tarp with something large under it. Three more tarps were scattered around nearby with things under them as well. These ones I knew didn't have Lord DeRom because the feet sticking out from under them were wearing human-made boots.

"Those three are vampires, Taxiss Clan. Looks like he gave as well as he took. We figure there must have been at least a dozen of them. Why they decided to take him in Son form instead of just waiting and taking his Host is a mystery. They must have been surprised by him or they needed him to be in Son form to do something for them, likely open a portal. Lord DeRom is here. You really shouldn't see this..." Karl said. Mike rarely spoke at all, and when he did, it was deeply accented in some foreign tongue that sounded like Natasha's accent but not quite. Natasha said it was one of the older Russian dialects from the north.

Dad walked up to the tarp and pulled it back some. He sobbed and turned away, then turned back and forced himself to see it. I took a step towards it as well and seen a white-furred ear sticking up out of a bloody mass. I couldn't make myself see anymore.

Dad put his hand on him and bowed his head and said something that could have been a prayer. I couldn't hear it exactly, but when he got up he looked like he had just been in a war or something from the look of his face. He seemed to have aged a decade in an instant.

"It's him. Those fuckers... they... I want them all dead. Kill every last fucking one of them. Wipe them off the Earth." He said and Karl nodded and put his big hand on Dad's shoulder. I didn't know if Mike and Karl were Son Host's or not, but I suspected they could have been Alphas from their appearance. Alphas tended to be very solidly built folks.

"What are we to do with the body?" Karl asked Dad. Dad looked at us then back at Karl and Mike with confusion. "I don't know... I guess I figured he wouldn't be in Son form if he died... I thought they were supposed to revert to human form when they died. Why didn't he change back? Do we notify his family or anything?"

Karl shook his head. "No family left that are not Allied. In situations like this, where Son's body is found and has not reverted back to its human form, it is only persons who are in the know that are permitted to take part in the funeral rights. We'll need to cremate him and turn the bones to dust. Have any of you taken part in Son funerals before?"

We all shook our heads no. It was a topic we had never really gotten into. I just assumed they buried or cremated the bodies and put up a marker of some sort. We never discussed the possibility of him dying in Son form and not changing back. He had no clue how to proceed.

"Son funerals are usually several days long. How old was he?" Karl asked us.

"Thirty-five… almost thirty-six." I said.

"Ok, so let's see... three days for the thirty and a day for each year under ten makes five, so eight days we need to display and mourn him. If he was forty, it would be four days, but if he was thirty-nine, it would be twelve. Every decade is a day and every year is a day. Get it?" he said and we nodded.

"Also, most Son families hang their dead up, to appear standing. Eyes are kept open. Stories are said about the dead, usually just whatever stories the grieving feels like sharing. For the eight days, there will be much feasting, and someone has to be with the body all the time. It is never to be left alone. After the ceremony, if performed, we will burn him. Ashes will be kept, buried or scattered, or all three. It is customary for family and close friends to keep a small pouch of ashes, but the rest is generally scattered. We will request some be taken back with us to be put in the Council Chambers. We have ashes from pretty much all the DeRom Emperors there, at least from the ancient days. His will join them."

"So what do we tell people about Rob? People are going to wonder where he went." Dad asked Karl.

"After we leave, you may tell people that he said he never said anything to you. We will make it look as if he just moved away and got in an accident. We will send someone to go through his things. We found his will. It will be honored. It will take a while to process it all, though, to avoid suspicion."

Dad nodded and Karl and Mike remained with the body while Dad, Natasha, and I left. We got home and went into the house to tell Mom the news.

****

The ceremony was long, but we all stayed as long as we could afford to. Due to the damage that had been incurred to the body, it was not able to be propped up and displayed according to custom, but instead we elevated it on a bed of large logs until it was about six feet off the ground with piles of wood underneath it. It was wrapped tightly in a heavy canvas cloth and regularly doused with kerosene to keep the carrion eaters away from the body and also to help burn him when the time came.

Numerous stories were told about Lord DeRom and Rob; funny ones, sad ones, disturbing ones, and enlightening ones, and after eight days of stories, pigging out, being up all night, crying over our loss and laughing over our memories, we set him ablaze.

The fire burned a long time, about two days really, and Karl, Dad, and Mike took care of it exclusively. We were told it had to be done by those of his own gender. They returned with several cans of ashes, and we all took a pouch of it for ourselves and spread the rest of them around his place and the woods out back, as well as some at our place as well. Karl and Mike took a soda pop-sized can back with them as well, and after a short goodbye, they were gone as quickly as they had come.

Chapter Nine
The Trim

Jesse was a mess. He couldn't eat or sleep without seeing Natasha's face in his mind. He hadn't even been able to have sex with his fiancé Cheryl, or any of the other girls he had on the side. He thought of Natasha night and day, and when she finally did call him, he almost cried from joy.

They went out that night, and she had given him a kiss that had actually made him go off in his pants. He wanted her more than he ever wanted anyone else in his life, a thousand times more than Cheryl even, but she still wouldn't let him have her unless he was circumcised.

She wouldn't let him have her if she knew he was engaged or involved with other women either, but if she didn't know that little fact, then he wouldn't tell her. He wasn't sure what he would do if she did find it out, though. It would be a hard call.

He tried everything with the blonde bombshell. He took her to the fanciest restaurants on the island, he took her to plays and movies that he couldn't understand and fought to stay awake through, and he pried her with bottle after bottle of champagne that cost more than a day's wages a piece. But still, she wouldn't have sex with him.

He even spiked her drink a few times, but she just shook off the effects of the Rohypnol and asked for another glass. He was losing his mind, but he absolutely had to have her. She was the absolute *masterpiece* of femininity. There wasn't a girl on the island that looked half as good as her, heck, she was better looking than the girls in Hollywood, and if he could get her, then everyone else would see him as the best man.

The thing was, he couldn't get her. He found her talking to other guys all the time and when he would get mad or ask her about them, she would just laugh and say that she didn't have a ring on her finger.

He eventually dumped the other girls he had going on the side. He couldn't afford to keep them. Natasha's tastes were extravagant and if he wanted to ever sink into that incredible body of hers, he needed to keep her happy. He couldn't risk having her see him with other girls, since she'd then expect to be with other guys.

He worked extra shifts at his job to help pay for it all. Cheryl was getting suspicious of him. She knew he slept with other girls from time to time, she didn't care. She liked it actually because it made her feel superior when they knew he belonged to her, but he never told her about this new girl, and when she had finally seen her, she panicked because she knew she was now very much outclassed.

Cheryl made his life a living hell, trying to get him to dump the others and be loyal for once, but he couldn't do it just yet. He *had* to have sex with the hot foreigner, he just had to, but until he did, she'd own him.

After a few more dates with Natasha, and several close calls with having sex, he decided to dump Cheryl for good if he wanted to ever get inside the foreign blonde Goddess.

Cheryl was devastated and decided to take it out on him by spreading rumors about him and hitting him for child support. Once she succeeded, several other girls hit him with it, too. He was in court for weeks getting things settled out, and by the time it was over, he was hopelessly in debt. But he was optimistic still. Natasha had found out he had been engaged and had a few kids with other girls and she had stayed interested in him regardless. He figured that any day now, those kisses of hers and the hungry stroking on the crotch of his pants would lead to her surrender and he would get her. But every time she came close, had his manhood in her hands, she'd just look at it and shake her head.

"You need to be circumcised... I just can't do it with a man that's not. I'm sorry honey." She'd say and he'd go home with a case of blue balls that would drive him nuts half the night.

He seriously considered raping her, just forcing her down and taking what he wanted, but it wouldn't work. She had to be willing for him to feel like he won. Getting her stoned or drunk was one thing, but out and out force just wouldn't do. Besides, if she charged him and he went to prison for rape, HE'D get raped, and that wasn't something he liked the thought of. Jail for a few months he could handle, he had been in jail dozens of times already, but he was too pretty for years in an actual prison. They'd eat him alive in there.

After seeing nobody but Natasha for almost two months, he finally went and got himself circumcised. He needed to avoid seeing Natasha until he was healed up though. It hurt like crazy, and itched like the devil, and he was as weak as a baby for a few days afterwards, but he finally had it done. There was no reason now for her not to. No reason at all. He'd get her now. He was sure of it.

****

Steve and Eliza were boarding up Rob's house and shutting off the power and water when a rental car pulled into the laneway. It was Karl and Mike.

"Hey! Good to see you both again!" Steve said to the two large men as they got out of the car and came towards him. Steve stuck out his hand and shook hands with Karl, and then Mike.

"We tried calling a few times, but the line is cut here. His cell phone is missing too, likely in his shift bag with the clothes he was wearing that night." They said. Steve nodded.

"Yeah, we disconnected everything the other week and we're just here locking the place down. We cleaned everything up and went through everything with a fine-toothed comb to get rid of any Allied information he might have had lying around in case anyone comes around. He didn't have much left other than the stuff you guys took with you last time. He always made sure to tell me what to do with Allied stuff he had. All I found that was a few notebooks tucked away in the safe, but it was just his personal thoughts and stuff, nothing overly serious. I burned them, just to be on the safe side."

Karl scanned the kitchen and living room approvingly. "You seem to have done a good job. The place looks fine." He said. Mike just looked around at everything, nodding.

"He didn't really have much of anything really strange. He said something recently about having a rare artifact come into his possession from his barber of all people, something ancient and dangerous apparently, but he must have sent it to the Son Council already because it wasn't in his safe. I looked up the barber. Apparently, he recently died while on vacation in Egypt."

"Any word on what the artifact was?" Mike asked Dad.

Steve shook his head. "No. As I said, there was a folder with some notebooks with a bunch of personal information in it, but it was locked in a safe with my name on it. It was just the deed to the property and other banking stuff. Nothing else was in it. He had given me the combination years ago and told me that if he died, I was to open it. There was no mention of any artifact, though."

Karl let it go at that. Steve didn't want to go into any more detail than that. It was personal stuff Rob had entrusted to him to take care of, and he had, it wasn't Council or anyone else's business. Karl and Mike apparently agreed.

"The reason I came here is to tell you that we found several members of the Taxiss clan. They did not confess to having done anything to Lord DeRom and seemed as surprised as we were, but it could be a ruse. Falcon, one of their warriors, is reported to be coming here, though, so we thought we would warn you. He was the last vampire to speak to Lord DeRom and the main suspect in his death. We believe your daughter was present at the time they met."

"Yes, Jackette was his Aide," Steve said to him. "She went with him to Ireland to discuss something. Apparently, from what we were told, the meeting went well and they left on good terms."

"Well, apparently, the terms have changed. Falcon Taxiss and his minions are waging a rebellion against their superiors and have been for quite some time. We were informed that this Falcon is more than likely the mastermind of Lord DeRom's murder, probably in an attempt to get Son technology or to use him to open a portal somewhere only he could get to. We have orders to capture this Falcon and bring him in for questioning. Truthfully though, I plan to see he never draws breath again."

"If he killed Lord DeRom and Rob, I will kill him myself," Steve said. "Lord DeRom saved my life, and his Host Rob was my best friend. He introduced me to my wife. He's like family to me. Closer than a lot of family actually. I want in."

"Fair enough," Karl said to Steve. Mike just looked at them both and nodded in agreement.

****

The three vampires ran through the muddy field as fast and as hard as they could. It was late October now, and the ground was sloppy and hard to run in, but there was a thicket of trees a half mile ahead and they wanted to get to it before anyone seen them.

They had traveled a long way. They had stowed away on a cargo ship crossing the Atlantic and had been stealing rides on trains and transport trucks all the way from Halifax harbor to Prince Edward Island.

It was mid-afternoon, and it was a misty day, which only added to the misery of traveling on foot. They had exactly forty-two American dollars between the three of them when they left Ireland, and they were down to just over twenty-five now. They knew that the Sons were chasing them, but they had not seen or heard anything since they left Ireland. But they knew without a doubt they were being pursued by Sons. The "Sisters of Slaughter" to be precise.

They knew this because when they had left Ireland there were eight of them. One by one, the other five had been hauled away and massacred, and not always in the dead of night or even away from human eyes. Two of their group had suddenly vanished before their eyes in downtown Halifax yesterday afternoon, only to reappear a few seconds later in a nearby alley torn to shreds. Falcon and his two remaining friends didn't stick around long enough to see more. Three humans had witnessed the disappearing act and subsequent reappearance of the mangled bodies. Falcon had no clue what had happened to the human witnesses, but he doubted that they lived very long.

"I have to sleep." One of the vampires said to Falcon as soon as they had gotten into the little thicket of evergreens. He was young, no more than eighteen years old, and his older brother had been one of the ones to die in Halifax. "I haven't slept in four days now. I'm wiped. Just a bit. I beg you."

None of them had slept in four days. They couldn't risk it. Every time they stopped moving meant that their pursuers were getting closer to them. They had slowed down a bit in Halifax, and it had cost them two more lives. They couldn't risk any more long stops, there were only three of them left and they were almost at their destination. It would be vexing to die so close to their goal.

"Sleep, both of you. I'll keep watch as best I can." Falcon told the two others. They immediately made themselves as comfortable as they could on the wet cold ground and within seconds were out cold.

Falcon shivered so hard his teeth rattled. He had half a pack of matches left in his pocket but he was scared to use them to start a fire. Fire meant smoke, and smoke would be easy for their pursuers to detect.

He started a fire anyway. He had to. He doubted it would matter much. They had managed to find him and his group even when they didn't have a fire going, so he didn't figure it mattered now if he lit a small one. They were all soaking wet from sweat and mist and freezing from riding on the back of transport trucks for the last while. Canada was a lot colder than Ireland was in October.

He let the two others sleep for two hours while he got the fire going and heated up some food. They were in human form, and while it physically slowed them down and deadened their senses by half, it allowed them to walk amongst the humans without suspicion, as well as eat their food. They had to stay in human form. If they went into vampire form, the Sisters could detect them easier. Falcon wasn't sure how they could, just that they could. They had learned that the hard way back in Ireland before they managed to get on the cargo ship.

He prayed over his meal and then ate his share of the pack of ramen noodles he had cooked and then woke the other two up.

"Eat, this is for both of you. Share it." He told them as he lay down on a pile of old leaves he had heaped up under himself by the fire.

"I need to rest too. Keep the fire small and don't go anywhere in the open. Wake me up in half an hour. We need to get there before the Sisters catch us."

"I don't know why we are even bothering." One of the others said as he swallowed his share of the warm noodles and drank half of the broth before handing it to the other one.

Falcon looked at him sternly and the other one stared at the ground apologetically. "Because I said we must is why. Now, wake me up in an hour. We will find Jackette, the Aide, before nightfall."

"You had better hope we do." The other vampire said while the younger one gulped his meagre share of the food down greedily.

"Because if we don't, I doubt any of us will be alive by tomorrow."

****

"He got it done!" Natasha said to me as soon as she got in the house. She was laughing so hard she could barely talk. She had been in Charlottetown working on the last pieces of her immigration duties and had phoned Jesse from her usual pay phone in Summerside on her way back home. He didn't tell her, but rather, it was Jesse's mother. He was living with his mother in her basement in Summerside, and pretty much every cent he made now was going to support some of his various children.

"Who got what done?" I asked her, starting to laugh too because she was just so hysterical at the moment. It was kind of infectious.

"Jesse!" she said and then made a scissor motion across her crotch. I gasped and then burst out laughing as well.

"Oh, and another thing, he broke up with Cheryl for good and now he's swamped paying child support. I think we should probably end his suffering and let him know I have no intentions of sleeping with him." She said with a grin. Her English was much better now, but she still had a thick accent.

I nodded. He had suffered enough. Rumors were spreading about him all over town, and he was the talk of the town with all his paternity suits coming against him. Seven at last count, and rumors of another three more on the way.

Natasha looked at the papers I was looking at, then looked at me seriously. "Are you going somewhere?" She asked me after seeing various flyers for colleges out west. I shrugged.

"Maybe. I was just thinking about going away to go to school. Do something with my life and what not. Ever since the Host and Lord DeRom passed away, I've been feeling... I dunno... bored. I was thinking of getting some education. Maybe something political or something."

"Politics?" she asked and I nodded. "Yeah, I figure since I have some experience with it, I might have a bit of an advantage. I realize it's a different type of politics and everything, but still, it might help somewhat."

"What about me?" she asked and looked at me sadly. I looked back at her and immediately felt bad. I couldn't just uproot her again after having her move out here and getting her all settled in with Mom and Dad. She was family now.

"Well, you can come too! I was thinking we could both go. You could get into modelling or acting easily with your looks, and some of these schools have courses for both of us. We might even be able to share a dorm room or get an apartment of campus or something."

She frowned. "I don't know... I am happy here. This is the first real home I've ever had." She said. I knew she loved it here. From what few stories she had told me of her youth, she never really had much of a home life. She never told many stories of her youth at all, actually. I suspected it wasn't very fun.

"We'd just be going away for a few years, get out on our own. Get an education. We can't just sit around here and work on the farm our whole lives. Well, we could, but still. I need a change of scenery. It... just hurts too much being here now. Every time I look down the road, I think of him. I need to get away from here for a while."

Natasha was about to speak when there was a knock on the door. I looked out the window but there was no car in the laneway that I could see. I went to the door and opened it and then screamed.

Chapter Ten

Visitors

Falcon was standing there on my doorstep with two other guys. He was in human form, but I could still recognize him easily. I tried slamming the door, but he caught it before I could. I turned to run, but I felt a hand grab my arm. I screamed and fought, but it was useless. Natasha came running out and tried to attack them with the broom, but they flung something at her that knocked her cold, it looked like a little lasso with some type of hook on it that must have been coated with some type of drug. Falcon lay on top of me, pinning me to the floor. I expected him to rape me, than to kill me.

"Jackette! Jackette! We did not kill him! I swear to you we did not kill him! We have been framed! Jackette! Please calm down! Listen to me. I would not have come here if we were guilty would I? We have travelled all this way, please hear me out!"

It took a while for the panic to subside and his words to sink in. A part of me believed him, but I still didn't trust him as far as I could throw him.

"Why did you kill Lord DeRom?" I demanded and he shook his head.

"We didn't! I swear to God that we never touched him. We liked the Emperor! You saw it! Our masters must have done it, to frame us to get the Sons to help them subdue us! Maybe the Sisters did it! All I know is that it was NOT us! Please, Please Jackette, you must believe me!"

He made a lot of sense. He had tears in his eyes and he was desperate. I could tell that they were worn out, too. He looked twenty pounds lighter than he did last time I seen him and ten years older, but that was when he was in vampire form… and he was thin then.

He let me up then after making me promise not to attack him or try to run away or anything. We went inside the house and shut the door, dragging poor unconscious Natasha in with us.

****

We sat at the table then while Natasha was placed on the couch in the corner to recover. Whatever they had nailed her with had dropped her like a stone.

"This is Silas and Jacob Taxiss, fellow soldiers fighting for my people's cause," Falcon said as he introduced the two guys with him. They were young-looking, no more than their early twenties, I figured. They looked positively famished and filthy. Silas was the older of the two and Jacob the younger.

"We are now being hunted by the "Sisters of Slaughter."

There were eight of us when we left Ireland to come here. We managed to get on a boat coming here, but we lost five of our band before and after we docked in Halifax. We have suffered much and risked everything to get here Jackette. To tell you the truth. We did not kill Lord DeRom." Falcon said.

"So why should I believe you?" I asked. He just shrugged. He had no real proof to say otherwise, just the fact that he had come here risking his life to tell me he didn't.

"Ok, say I believe you... which I might... if you guys didn't kill him, who did? We found a Taxiss dagger and three dead Taxiss along with Lord DeRom's body. It sure looks like your people did it."

He smiled. "And it looks a lot like somebody was trying to make it look like we did, don't you think?" I had to admit that it did.

"How could we even get here? We cannot open the portals. You know that. We had to stow away on a cargo ship and hide on trucks to get here. But our superiors, they have their own planes and no shortage of our dead bodies to leave lying around. The Sisters of Slaughter, they joined our cause like Lord DeRom said they might, and our masters suffered horrible losses at their hands, but they wouldn't stop at killing just them. Going into battle with them was the same as going into battle against them! They went into frenzies, killing everyone around them, either friend or foe." Falcon said sadly.

I was enthralled by what he was saying, and it was making a bit of sense. The Sisters were all rumored to be associated with the House of V'Lin. They couldn't just stop a slaughter once it started. They were best avoided in battle. I guess Falcon had learned that the hard way. He continued.

"They proved to be a bit too indiscriminate in their killing. We began suffering more casualties at their hands than we were at our masters. We started letting them go into battle alone, but that proved to be foolish of us to do. They won a huge victory over one of the Taxiss fortresses, one that apparently had a lot of knowledge in it, private information only our highest leaders would know, and then they refused us entry to it.

We had been trying to crack that place hundreds of times over the years and the Sisters just marched in and took it in hours. But after they took it, they wouldn't surrender it to us like we had agreed. They kept the information for themselves, said it was for our "best interest" and that it was confidential as it regarded "Son weapons and artifacts". We even told them that they could keep whatever Son information they found, that we just wanted the fortress, but they told us "no". After that, we severed our dealings with them, we tried to contact Lord DeRom, to tell him of the Sister's actions, but we couldn't reach him. We tried for days, but we were told that he was either dormant or dead... that his essence was not free and could not be reached. Then we started hearing stories that he was dead and that WE supposedly had done it. Once the Sisters heard that we were going to come here ourselves to meet with you, they began attacking us without mercy."

"But why would that anger them?" I asked him. It made no sense.

"We don't know! But whatever they discovered in that stronghold made them incredibly suspicious of everyone. I only know that it involved something that Lord DeRom was given by an Alliance archaeologist recently. They don't want us to have it for certain... and apparently, they didn't want Lord DeRom to have it either."

I grimaced. "Why would a group of Son fanatics want an artifact from being in the hands of their Ruler? Unless they plan on using it without his permission."

It was Falcon's turn to shrug. "I have no idea. But we had to come here to tell you the truth, but the Sisters have been hunting us every step of the way. I only thank almighty God that he allowed me to make it here to tell you the truth. You may kill me now if you wish. I only hope you can convince the Sisters to stop the slaughter of my people." He said and then sat down on the floor and hung his head.

"So you need me to persuade the Son Council to try to call off the Sisters and to tell them that you are innocent?" I said. Falcon nodded. I doubted that it would make any difference what Council told them. The Sisters were nuttier than squirrel turds. I wanted to believe him though, and a big part of me did, but I was still leery.

"She's waking up." The youngest looking vampire said as he sat next to Natasha. I went over to her to keep her calm as she woke.

"Don't panic. It's O.K. They're friends." I said to her as she looked at me with confusion and then terror, then finally confusion once again. I gave her the rundown of everything Falcon had told me.

"We should tell your parents." She said and I nodded. I looked at Falcon and he nodded as well.

Natasha passed me her cell phone, but I shook my head. "No cells. They are at Rob's house. We just had his phone disconnected. We'll have to go there in person." I told him and Falcon looked at me, trying to see if I was trying to lead him into a trap.

"You can go, but leave her here." He said, motioning to Natasha. She looked at me and shrugged in acceptance.

"O.K... but if you hurt her, so help me God, I'll convince the Son Council to end your entire race. They likely aren't very far from making that decision already."

"I know it," Falcon said softly. "We will not harm her, if you do not betray your word."

I left and went to Rob's house. It was weird going there without him. It was the first time I had went there since the funeral. It was hard.

I walked into the house and was confronted by Karl and Mike, they turned to face me and then smiled. "Jackette. Good to see you again. We have just received news on the killers. They are coming to the island. Do not worry. We are here to protect you." Karl said. Mike just nodded.

"I have news, too. I don't think the Taxiss killed Emperor DeRom, at least not the Taxiss we think did it." They looked at me strangely, as did Mom and Dad. I sat down and began relaying everything Falcon had said.

****

Jesse smashed his fist into the mirror, sending his reflection to a thousand pieces throughout the room. He had just found out his mother had told Natasha about his circumcision, and he was pissed off. He wanted to surprise her, but the old bat had to interfere in his business. She usually did and it was that reason that he usually didn't tell her anything.

He got in his car and drove around Summerside for hours, looking for Natasha. He wandered through every high-end store and restaurant he could find looking for her, then gave up and returned home frustrated. He had been driving himself crazy over this broad for months now and she still hadn't given him her home address or her phone number. He had dumped his fiancé over her, dumped his chicks on the side, took responsibility for his bastard children and worked himself to the bone working overtime just to buy her nice things, and he still hadn't gotten so much as a hand job from her! She wouldn't even suck it, for God's sake!

Well, she would now! She had no more excuses now! He'd have her every which way but Tuesday! No more excuses! She was going to give him what he wanted or by God, he'd take it by force! He didn't care anymore if he got busted for sexual assault. He'd wear a condom and get an alibi and it would be his word against hers, if she bothered to charge him. Hell, she might not need to be forced at all. She had always acted like she wanted to, but was just holding back cause of the whole circumcision thing. Well, there was no more reason not to now, and if she started with her bullshit reasons, he'd put an end to that crap real quick!

He got a phone call as soon as he walked in the door from

Claude Howard, a friend of his from St. Felix, up at the western end.

"Dude, I seen that hot blonde you're chasing. You're not going to believe who she's friends with!" Claude said to him.

"Who?" Jesse asked. He was expecting to hear a guy's name. He wasn't worried about any guys. He could steal any girl from any guy up west. He'd done it lots. Lots and lots.

"Jackette MacNeill," Claude said. Jesse was silent.

"They've been playing you, dude! Fucking you over big time! I saw them both driving around town a few times now and just figured it out that that foreign girl you're after and Jackette's friend are the same chick. You're right though, holy shit, she's smoking hot! Like some movie star or something."

Jesse felt his rage rising. He'd been played. The same way he had played other people, including Jackette, he had been played. The bitches had made him get his foreskin cut off, which hurt like hell for days, and had cost him a shit load of money too... and they had cost him a lot of good times with other girls, too. Well, he'd fix that! He'd rape both of them.

He hung the phone up and hopped in his car after packing a bag with some clothes. "Going up west for a few days to see Claude." He yelled to his folks as he walked out the door without hearing what they had to say about it.

He got in his car and started it, then sat behind the wheel. He'd fuck her for sure now. Fuck her good and Jackette too, just for spite. And he'd get away with it. He'd make sure of that. He'd sneak over and get them by surprise or something. No foreign bitch was going to get away with fucking him over like that. No one was.

****

Falcon explained the entire thing out to Mike and Karl and Jackette's parents as they stood in the kitchen of the MacNeill house. He did so very nervously, because both Karl and Mike had very large caliber handguns aimed at his head.

They lowered them when he had finished. Falcon exhaled deeply. He may have been considered an assassin, but these two were Son-trained enforcers called "Dark Angels". He could carry out the odd execution or killing for his vampire masters; but these two would destroy whole towns. He had heard rumors of "Dark Angels" before. Usually non-shifters, but often high bloods or even Alphas, they sometimes even had some of Son's mental abilities and more than one trick up their sleeves.

Most of them came from either the Wara family and due to the Wara's black fur and ties to the Son church, the enforcers were called "Dark Angels." All his life, he had never seen anyone of his people meet a "Dark Angel" and live to tell the tale, and now he was dealing with two of them.

"So... what do you want us to do?" Falcon asked Karl, who looked at Mike briefly before answering. His life and the lives of his entire race were at stake. He only hoped that the "Dark Angels" supposed ability to determine truth from lies was working.

"Aside from bathe, nothing," Karl said with a frown. Falcon and his two young companions stunk. Badly.

"We need to find out if the Sisters of Slaughter killed Lord DeRom and what this artifact they are after does," Karl said after a bit. "I will tell the Council that you have no knowledge of his death and have acted with honor. This might even make the Sisters stop coming after you... now that you've already spilled the beans."

"I would appreciate that a great deal," Falcon said with a look of relief. His two friends looked like large weights were lifted off of them as well.

"But now we still have no clue as to what the Sisters want with this artifact... and what did the Taxiss have to do with it. What do they know about Son artifacts?" Dad said. Karl looked at him and shook his head.

"We need to capture a Taxiss superior and question them,"

Karl replied.

Falcon looked at him and winced. "Esau, the leader, is almost always at sea. You cannot portal to a moving point, or even a floating point, this much we know. It was the only way we avoided the Sisters coming here by sea. Once we hit land, we had to keep moving all the time. Many of our wealthier people prefer a life at sea for this reason."

Karl nodded. "True, you cannot portal to a moving point, but we don't necessarily need Esau himself. We just need a high end member of the Taxiss Clan that knew what was going on at that compound. If we can speak to them, I can tell if they are lying."

Falcon spoke again. "They are usually all under severe security. The Sisters themselves said that they had impressive security. Infrared sensors, laser detection grids, heat detectors, motion detectors, snipers, landmines... you name it, they have it. They don't want visitors, Son or otherwise, and have taken every precaution against them. Short of levelling most of Ireland or Boston with a nuclear device, or go sinking hundreds of armed yachts, you're not going to touch any of them."

"Trust me, technology has weaknesses like anything else. You say that the Sisters now have in their possession a Bar'Ka'Nofa helmet they stole from the fortress. It can amplify their mental abilities. Likely, it is how they were able to open portals. Only their leader could open them before. The only reason that the vampires haven't had any Sisters visit before is because the Sisters never wanted to visit." Karl said. "I'll ask around and see if anyone knows anything about it."

Mom jumped in then. "Well, we can't do anything if we're starving. Steve, see if you have anything in your closet that will fit Mr. Falcon and his two friends here while I cook up something for us to eat and they have a nice hot bath. We'll need to get these three boys that drink Rob made to negate the effects of his land on vampires. We can't have them getting sick of us. I think I seen it in his box of things we put upstairs. I also think it would be wise if we all stayed here tonight... just in case somebody comes looking for trouble."

Karl looked at Mike, who just shrugged in agreement to Mom's suggestion. "Very well," Karl said. "If it's no inconvenience to you and your family."

"Inconvenience? It's a might more inconvenient to be killed by whoever killed Rob and Lord DeRom than it is to have friends stay the night. Now, don't be silly and go get your things. Jackette will help you find your way around and show you to a room to stay in." Mom said with determination.

The two large men just nodded and then went out to their car and came back a few minutes later with a large bag each. From the sound they made when they were set down on the floor, it wasn't clothing inside, unless they wore a lot of clothes made from gun barrel metal.

While Karl and Mike were getting their things ready, Natasha was in charge of getting the vampires settled. Dad had brought them the potion that negated the effects of Son blessed lands and the three vampire males were more than eager to drink it before they became deathly ill. Each shape-shifting race had its own type of energy field that encompassed its grounds. The energy often had harsh side effects on other shifters. There were certain ways to counteract the effects, and Rob had made and stored a goodly supply of it years ago when he was dating a vampire girl so she could come by.

Steve also handed out each of the vampires a set of his old clothes. Nothing spectacular by any stretch, just some old t-shirts and pants, but the vampires stared at them like they were gold. Their old clothing seemed to almost consist entirely of patches.

Mom and I cooked supper, throwing a bit of everything we had on the stove. By the time everyone had been cleaned up and settled, we had a good-sized meal ready.

The vampires all bowed their heads and prayed before eating, then ate like there was no tomorrow. Karl and Mike both ate surprisingly little for such large men, only eating about the same as

Natasha or I would. The vampires occasionally wept as they ate, enjoying the home-cooked meal so much that it brought them to tears. I felt a pang of sympathy for them at the miserable lives they must have had endured to be brought to tears over pork chops and mashed potatoes.

Chapter Eleven
The Sisters

The Sisters of Slaughter had split up physically, but mentally, they were still able to communicate as if they were side by side. There were only seven of them now. One sister had been hit by a train leaping for a vampire who had scrambled away from her across a subway track. She had been overzealous and had miscalculated her jump. That miscalculation had resulted in her death, which only made the remaining Sisters more motivated to catch the vampires.

They were in two groups now, with all but one of them chasing the vampires to the DeRom grounds on Prince Edward Island and the remaining one, their leader Ma'Gora V'Lin, staying in the vampire fortress in Ireland. She had more important things to do.

The Bar'Ka'Nofa helmet had saved them a lot of trouble. Of all the Sisters, she alone could open a portal. However, upon finding the helmet in the vampire's fortress, she was able to remain behind while one of the other sisters used the helmet to open the portals, leaving her to do other things. And since she was the mentally most powerful one of the group, she had other things to do. Important things.

The Taxiss had gotten the information from their spies in the Grand Alliance. Both Sons and vampires had spies in each other's camps, some were even known to be double agents, and sometimes these double agents even served as liaisons' between the two cultures. There was no war going on between the Sons and the vampires, after all.

The Sisters learned little else after raiding the Taxiss stronghold. Many secrets the vampires had accumulated over the years were useless or common knowledge for most Sons. However, it was the report from a double agent telling of a recent find of a powerful artifact found off the coast of Egypt once possessed by the O'Sian's called the "moonstone" that caught Ma'Gora's attention. It was said to be an ancient O'Sian artifact that was used to collect astral power in. She had of course, heard all about astral power and how it was used to power the O'Sian devices left behind. Powerful devices. Very powerful. As in, destroy whatever and whomever you want. Like the entire vampire or human race. With the helmet, she could begin to access that power.

Only the most powerful members of Son society knew anything about using and controlling astral power. The DeRom were said to be the masters of it. The report said that the "moonstone" had been found during an underwater dig in the Mediterranean Sea. The dig was Alliance run, the finds would not be for the public, and that the moonstone was found in a secured area of an ancient temple complex and almost had been in vampire hands.

It was whispered that those who had the "moonstone" could imprison the soul of anyone. Whatever souls imprisoned could then be harvested for their astral energy, giving the possessor great powers. It was possibly a prison for thousands of souls the O'Sian's would have considered evil, and those that controlled the stone could use the power of those souls to open powerful portals to wherever and it was rumored, whenever they wished, or to even leave the Earth entirely… possibly even back to the O'Sian home world. Of course, they would also power the powerful but lifeless tools the O'Sian's left behind. It would be the ultimate weapon.

The Sisters wanted that stone, and they wanted it badly.

"They are on DeRom land! Search the whole of his island for them and slay them. Make them suffer! Bring back the moonstone! It must not fall into anyone else's hands! Slay all who oppose you!" the voice of Ma'Gora V'Lin, who was back in Ireland, said to the minds of the Sisters who had followed the vampires to Canada.

They acknowledged her commands and ran on a beeline course right down the middle of the Route Two main highway, zigzagging around cars driven by people who couldn't see them. They were masking, a trick similar to charming except more effective, and only able to be done by two or more Sons at a time, which rendered a selected area or item totally invisible in a mental bubble. The only people that could see through the masking trick were very small children, and the severely mentally unstable or highly impaired. Sometimes, the ravings of drunk lunatics or little kids were actually truths in disguise.

The Sisters needed no map, although none of them had ever been on the island before. Every Son knew the DeRom's territory. They could sense it as surely as migrating birds know where south is or how a salmon can find the exact stream they were born in. They just knew where it was and they were going there as fast as their strong legs could take them.

The Sister running furthest to the right lifted her head and then tore off through a freshly harvested potato field. The other Sisters followed her, trusting her instincts without questioning, and already knew what she had sensed. She had picked up a scent of their vampire prey.

They arrived where Falcon and his two friends had made camp for a few hours. "They were here. They ate and slept, then they left again, going west." One of the Sisters said to the others. Every one of the Sisters, both here and back in Ireland, knew what she had seen, smelled, and said. They were hive-minded in a way, able to block others if they wished, but able to join in an astral realm where communication was wide open. Any Son could communicate with any other, if they were allowing contact. Most of the time it was just used by individuals who knew one another. Rarely was it ever used to communicate to everyone at once, but it could be done if one was strong enough mentally to do so. Few were.

"How long ago?" one of the Sisters asked her. She sniffed the ground and then felt the ashes of the fire. "Yesterday, around this time. They have undoubtedly found the home of Lord DeRom's Host by now and may already have the moonstone. Orders?" the Sister named Karraka V'Lin, who had found the vampire's scent, asked of her leader back in Ireland.

"Find them and slaughter them. If it is not found with them, then go to the home of his Allies. They will have likely already emptied his home of anything of value. We do know that it has not been given to the Council. Go to them and get the moonstone! Kill whomever and however you wish. The recovery and delivery of the moonstone to me is our number one priority." Ma'Gora said.

"We are no more than two hours from there. We will contact you once we get there." The Sisters on the island told Ma'Gora and then closed their minds so they could better focus on masking and resumed running west. Always to the west.

****

I sat with Natasha in my room, talking, when our landline phone rang. I picked it up without looking at the number and regretted not having a cell phone. It was Jesse.

"You fucking bitches! You happy now, Jackette? Huh? You have a good laugh at me? You little fucking cunt! Is Natasha there with you? Put her on." He demanded. He had called a few times so far, threatening us, but he hadn't shown up yet. He was still scared of Dad's shotgun. I could only imagine what he would do if he seen Mike and Karl coming after him, or even Falcon, for that matter. Mike and Karl could crush his skull like an empty beer can. Falcon could just shift and drink him dry like one.

I handed the phone to Natasha, who laughed and took the receiver from me. "Yes?" she said sweetly and I could hear Jesse cursing at her from the other end. Natasha just looked at me and laughed silently, listening to Jesse freaking out at her.

He had gone through a whole series of emotions since he started calling us. He had tried sweet talking, demanding, crying, swearing, being apologetic, and was now back at demanding. The only reason he wouldn't come by was because Dad had shot his car the last time he was here.

Jesse had apparently ranted and raved himself out and was back to crying again. Natasha was sweet-talking him, telling him that she really did care for him and everything, getting his hopes all up, then told him that she'd love him if only he'd cut his balls off and mail them to us. Jesse would go back into another tirade and Natasha would laugh at him some more. Sometimes, she would hang up on him, other times, she'd let him talk for a bit. Either way, she always mocked him.

"I'm gonna go over there! So help me, God woman, I'm gonna go over there and you and Jackette won't like it!" he said at last, then hung up on her. Natasha hung the phone up and rolled her eyes.

"Apparently, he's coming over and we won't like it." She said nonchalantly. I wasn't overly worried about him coming over here acting tough. We had two Dark Angels, two regular vampires, a vampire assassin, and enough high-end weaponry that would make a Navy Seal go off in his pants. Jesse would be lucky if he only had Dad and his old twelve gauge to deal with this time.

Dad yelled up to me. "Jesse gonna kill us all again?" he asked with a laugh. He hadn't threatened to do anything like that yet, but he did threaten to punch out Dad the next time he seen him. Considering Dad was now carrying a Son handgun that would hit you with an energy bolt equivalent to two bolts of lightning, I didn't think he was overly worried.

"Yeah. He says he's coming over again too. You guys might

want to keep your eyes open for him if he does come by." I yelled down to him and he laughed.

Natasha looked at me and then grinned. "I think Falcon likes me." She said and I rolled my eyes. Natasha was currently infatuated with Falcon and the vampire seemed to be somewhat interested in her as well. Oddly enough though, the three vampire men had taken strongly to Mom, following her around like lapdogs, constantly doing everything in their power to make her more comfortable. She had been feeding them everything under the sun and they had been eating it and appreciating it as well. Mom only had to say she was going to go do something out in the barn or around the house and one of the three vampire men would jump to do it for her. I figured it was because they probably never had much interaction with women other than vampire girls who were objects for sex and little more. They were craving mothers.

Dad and Karl were fast friends now. Dad had found out that Karl liked the odd drink or two in the evening and so now, after supper for the last two nights, they would sit back and have a few shots of Dad's homebrew. Mike had tried a drink or two of it as well, but tended to be more of a loner, spending his time scanning for life signs with some fancy scanner he had, and cleaning his weapons. He still rarely ever spoke. He seemed to be all business, with the exception of reading arm wrestling and trapping magazines.

Natasha and I just tried to stay out of everyone's way. We helped out when and how we could, but most of the time, we just stayed up in my room and watched movies online or something. Neither of us were exceptional marksmen, so they gave us each a large butcher knife to use if we needed it.

The phone rang again, this time saying an unknown name, unknown number. Jesse again no doubt, this time getting smart and hiding the call display. I answered it with an annoyed "Hello?"

"Is this the MacNeill residence?" A strangely accented voice asked me. The caller sounded as if he was older, like in his seventies or eighties.

"Yes?" I said curiously but inquisitively, waving my hand at Natasha to put our show on pause.

"I am looking for a Mr. Steven MacNeill. Might I speak with him for a moment?" The voice asked me politely.

"May I ask who is calling?" I asked, curious. He sounded old and creepy.

"Of course. My name is Esau Taxiss." The voice said on the other end. My blood ran cold.

"I'll tell him to pick up, Mr. Taxiss. Hold for a moment, please." I told him nervously, then set the phone on the bed softly and gave Natasha a look of panic. She stared at the phone curiously, a look of concern on her face.

I ran downstairs and told Dad that Esau Taxiss was on the landline. Dad looked at Karl, who just reached over and handed him the phone. Dad picked it up with Karl listening in beside him, while I ran back upstairs and listened in with Natasha.

"Hello?" Dad said politely. "Mr. Taxiss? How may I help you?"

"Mr. MacNeill?" the old man said. He sounded like he was Eastern European. "Are you an employee of Mr. DeRom?"

"Yes," Dad replied. Now everybody knew who and what everybody was. Good.

"Mr. MacNeill... some lady employees of Mr. DeRom, members of his company, moved into one of my houses the other day, and these ladies as well as some of my former employees have caused me great pains as of late. I was informed that some of these lady friends and some of these rogue employees of mine were headed your way, possibly to pay an unwanted visit to Mr. DeRom."

"I see," Dad said. "And what do you want me to tell him?"

"This is a friendly warning to him. I'm told they may wish to cause him harm. I am trying to smooth over ruffled feathers, as it were by sending him this information. I am told these ladies are no longer working for the best interest of anyone but themselves. I'm also led to believe that there are a small number of my previous employees possibly travelling with them. I would advise dealing with them in an extreme way as well. Do what you wish with them. I will consider it a kindness on your part if they are dealt with sternly." Old Esau said in a controlled tone.

"I'll be sure to tell him. For your information, Mr. DeRom did *not* endorse these lady friends of his to interfere with your organization, he only advised your employees that his organization would not get involved and that they may agree to help. They are acting on their own. I'm sure he wants no troubles between either of your... companies. As for your employee however, there are several that are now working for Mr. DeRom's organization and are now valued members of our team. Perhaps you should have offered them a better benefit package while they were on strike?" Dad said back to him and I fought to keep from laughing. I had no idea Dad was that sharp. Speaking in code like that could be tricky if you weren't a quick thinker.

"I see. Well, either way, as long as no more of my employees leave, I will allow them and their immediate families to retain their current... life insurance benefits. Might I enquire as to how many of them joined your organization?"

"Three of them. One of your lower managers and two of his subordinates. They are currently speaking to two of my organizations... public relations experts… that are right here as we speak. You can thank them for preventing... a hostile takeover... of your business. It appears that your former employees had problems with these lady friends you mentioned as well, and are no longer working together. These ladies you mention are no longer members of our company, nor have they been for some time. You have our permission to do as you see fit with them."

"I believe I understand. Very well, Mr. MacNeill. I thank you for these negotiations. I'd like to have this all back to the way it was... as well as his word in writing. If he would be willing to sign a deal, I would sign as well. Would he be available to talk?" The old vampire Lord said. He was asking for a formal truce.

"Well, Mr. Taxiss, these lady friends you speak of are freelance clients. They are not acting on our organization's behalf, so we'll leave you two to hammer out whatever negotiations suit you both best. Mr. DeRom is indisposed at the moment and cannot take your call. We do appreciate your call though, and hope you and these ladies settle your disagreement. We will be on the lookout for them as well if they attempt anything unsavory here. We do hope they move out of that house of yours. We appreciate the warning as to their intentions as well. If there are any other future misunderstandings, be assured, we will deal with them in whatever would be the best course of action for mutual growth and benefit to both our companies."

"I would appreciate that as well." The old vampire said. He sounded relieved.

"Is there any other business you care to discuss today?" Dad asked him politely. I had to commend him for his code skills. He was excellent at it. If anyone was listening in, they wouldn't think it was anything more than businessmen talking... at least as long as they weren't in the know. Anybody that did know the truth would have no troubles figuring it out.

"None," Esau said.

"Very well then, thank you for calling and have a nice day," Dad said and then hung up. Natasha and I were both downstairs seconds after.

Karl looked at Dad and then at everyone else. "Ok, Esau Taxiss just called and according to what he said, he has no idea that Lord DeRom is dead. I thought for sure that he was behind the murder... but I guess not. He didn't even seem to know about it and you didn't let him know either, which was good thinking on your part, Steve. Falcon, you, Silas and Jacob are no longer associated with the Taxiss. The old man said he won't harm your families and you're free. You can join our cause if you wish, but I would be unsure as to which family you could join since the DeRom are all dead now. We'll discuss that later. He didn't know how many of you made it here, which leads me to believe that these Sisters caused him a shit load of misery as well and he has little in the way of recent information. Now, from what we know now, since we know he didn't kill Lord DeRom, so who did?"

"I think the Sisters did it," I said. Everyone looked at me in disbelief. Ordinarily, no Son would ever dream of killing a DeRom. It would be pointless. The DeRom were the rulers, period. No other family could rule. The DeRom were the strongest mentally and they were designed by the O'Sian's to be the leaders. But the Sisters weren't associated with a family any more. They were mostly all V'Lin's by birth... a respected and noble family... but they were renegades now and no longer formally recognized by them. They hadn't been for years. They had such disregard for the rules that even the radical V'Lin family had washed their hands of them.

"We all know that only the DeRom are allowed to rule, and none of the other families would stand for some other family trying to change that. But the Sisters have no family ties anymore. Also, they are some of the only Sons able to kill him that would also have access to dead Taxiss bodies. Falcon said they killed a bunch of his people as well as the higher ranking Taxiss. The Sisters could have come through a portal and killed him easily. Lord DeRom was strong mentally, but if they surprised him, or all got to him at once, or tricked him somehow, or blackmailed him, they could have done it. If they are as militant as they are rumored to be, they might have seen Rob as too weak or figured to take control of the Alliance themselves or something. No family would do it, but they are outcasts in a way. Freelance operatives not associated with a family. The real question is why? Doing so would put every Son in existence out for vengeance on them. They must be after the artifact. It must be worth an awful lot to bother with all the risk."

Karl furrowed his brow. "There isn't a reason. We already have all the artifacts the DeRom had and there was nothing that looked even remotely like some big rock full of souls. There was nothing else there worth that risk. Nothing else he had would be of any value to them. I doubt the Sisters will try anything against our three orphans now, but I think we all should stay a few more days just to make sure the old leech isn't lying. I couldn't sense that he was lying, but it is tricky to tell over the phone. He might have the ability to hide that from us too, you never know. There could be a dozen vampires out there right now waiting to take us all out. I doubt it, but you can never tell a hundred percent. You never found anything else over at his place that you never told me about, did you?"

Dad looked at Karl and shook his head. "No, I swear it. I sent everything he had listed to where he had ordered it to be sent. We have nothing here. I think you guys should stay around another few days, though, just be sure." Karl and Mike both nodded.

"Somebody is here." One of the vampires said as he looked

out the window to see an Oldsmobile Cutlass Supreme pull into the laneway. "A blue Cutlass Supreme that looks like it was shot in the front fender."

"Oh shit!" I said. It was Jesse. Natasha blushed and looked at Falcon. Karl looked at Dad who just shook his head. "Just a neighborhood punk. He's sweet on the girls. Been hassling them a lot. He's the guy that keeps calling." Karl just rolled his eyes. Falcon looked jealous and slightly flushed.

Mike looked up and took his gun sights off of Jesse. He had some strange looking type of rifle that wasn't made by humans. It could still kill them easily enough, though.

I put my shoes on and went outside to talk to Jesse. He looked like shit.

"Jackette... is Natasha here?" he asked me. His voice was shaking and he seemed like he was ready to pop apart at the seams at any given moment.

"There she is now," I said to him as Natasha came out the door of the house. I could see Falcon staring at her through the curtains.

"Natasha... will you come for a drive with me? I gotta talk to you." He said desperately. She shook her head.

"I don't have to talk to you, Jesse." She said coolly. "I just gave you a taste of your own medicine. You used girls, used Jackette. You got her pregnant and didn't even care. If she hadn't miscarried, she'd have your child by now and you wouldn't care in the least. If I had let you have sex with me, you would have happily gotten me pregnant, too and you wouldn't have cared about me either. I let you feel a little bit of the pain you caused others."

Jesse nodded sadly. "I'm so sorry... I am. I'm sorry Jackette... I really am. I didn't want to get you pregnant... it just happened. But Natasha, it isn't like that with you. I love you. I had never loved anybody else before. Not even Cheryl."

Natasha just shrugged. "I don't love you Jesse. I never did. And I don't believe that you love me either. You don't know me. You're just in love with my wrapper… not my heart. I just wanted to teach you a lesson and let you feel some of the pain you made other girls feel."

Jesse put his head down then and cried. I actually felt sorry for him a bit, but he had it coming.

"So you don't love me... you never will love me?" he asked her and she just shook her head and giggled. God, she was heartless when she wanted to be. I loved it.

Jesse turned to look at me then. "So what about you Jackette? Do you hate me too?" he asked me. I shook my head.

"No, I don't hate you Jesse. I just hate what you did and how you did it." I told him. He nodded and then looked up at me.

"Think maybe you'd give me a second chance?" he asked. I wasn't sure if he was asking me or Natasha.

"What?" I asked him. "Are you asking ME if I want to go out with you again?" I asked him. He nodded and then shrugged. "Well... either of you." He said. I just rolled my eyes and turned to go back in the house. He was hopeless.

Natasha spoke to him for a few more minutes before coming back into the house as well. Jesse tore out of the laneway, yelling out insults. Falcon glared out the window at him as he drove away and I could tell that he was jealous.

"Good Lord, what an asshole!" she said with a laugh. Dad looked at her and asked what had happened between them and she told everyone the whole story. Everybody was laughing hard by the time she got to how she persuaded him to get circumcised, even the usually silent Mike.

****

"We have arrived at the DeRom's Host's house. There is nothing here that we can sense. The moonstone must be with his

Allies. Has he said anything else about it yet?" One of the Sisters said to their leader.

"Nothing but drunken nonsense. He said something about a grey Guardian and placing the moonstone on the moon, but I doubt that he would have a way of sending it that far away. We know of a few Temple Guardians, but none are grey." The head Sister said angrily. She had Rob in the Taxiss Fortress she now ruled, chained to a bed, feeding him an intravenous drip of alcohol to keep Lord DeRom dormant.

Keeping the Host permanently drunk was the only way to ensure the DeRom inside of him was unable to come forward enough to communicate with anyone, or even to know what was going on. But there were problems. She couldn't easily enter his mind with any real control while he was in that state, and she wouldn't dare do it if he was sober. She knew he had the moonstone, and what it was rumored to be capable of, she had gleaned that much from him at least, but as to its whereabouts, that was another matter.

She looked at him lying there on a hospital bed, with the tube going into his arm. He had been lying here for about two months now. She dared not kill him. Neither would the vampires if he somehow fell into their clutches. He would be much more useful to both parties alive, but only if she kept him in this state and only if she could get him to cooperate. So far, all he'd do would insult her, sing bawdy drinking songs, think of scenes from movies, and tell dirty jokes. But he was cracking. She knew that much. And once she had the moonstone, she could use it to gain control of the portals… ALL of the portals, and if the time travel thing was true, she would go back to when vampires were at their weakest and finish them off. Then she'd go really far back and see the O'Sian's when they were making the different races and she'd place the Sons as the rulers of the Earth, not just the observers. And as soon as the O'Sian's left she would lead them in battle to subdue and dominate the rest except the vampires. They had to go completely. And she knew which one she wanted to die first.

She'd have the vampires butchered to extinction, just for fun. She knew she wouldn't be able to wipe out all the humans, though. They were necessary. A world of Sons would die off in no time. The humans would be breeding stock basically, and servants. The first thing she would order would be to control the human population, leaving only the strong and healthy to survive. Next to go would be all the polluting power sources on earth. No cars, no planes, no trains, no electricity unless it was powered by clean tech. The age of the horse would be back, as would sailing ships. The Earth was a stinking cesspool of pollution and it was mostly due to there being too many human mouths to feed. Too much competitions led to greed and corruption, and that led to too much catering to weakness and laziness. She'd put a screaming halt to that bullshit. It'd all stop in an instant.

"I think I'll have the humans clean the forests... every forest on Earth. Get rid of all the old brush, thin out all the overcrowded stuff, and chop down everything that is diseased. Plant healthy stock in its place, and increase the amount of forested land tenfold." She thought happily. That was what bothered her most about the humans. They already knew what needed to be done, they just refused to do any real work on it. Forestry services were a joke as far as she was concerned. Human needs always outranked natures needs now. Well, she'd soon end that when she was Empress. She'd make the whole of North America primarily forest, just like it used to be, and to cut a tree down without permission would be a capital offence.

She checked the line feeding the Imperial Host alcohol. She had some difficulty keeping it in at times, since his sweat and the alcohol tended to unstick the glue of the tape holding it in him, but it was fine at the moment. He was out like a light. He passed out a lot. She figured she was feeding him a bit more alcohol than she should be really, but she didn't want to take any chances of having Lord DeRom come out of dormancy. If he came out before she had the moonstone... well... it wouldn't be a good thing. He'd crush her mind in an instant or tell everyone else where he was, what was going on, and who had done this. And if that happened, every Son and Alpha would be out for her and her Sister's throats in a New

York minute.

She put her hand on his head and entered his mind. Going inside wasn't the problem, it was getting out with anything meaningful that seemed to be the issue. He was either incredibly cunning, even while drunk, and was able to confuse his thoughts so much that nobody could hope to decipher them, or he was totally insane. She kind of figured it was a blend of both. The DeRom Host's tended to be that way. It was a miracle that she had even found out about the moonstone.

"How are you feeling?" She asked his unconsciousness. At once he began singing some old sea shanty and flooding his thoughts with images from various scenes from bars and pubs.

"The Moonstone given to you from the O'Sian's. Where is it? Is it safe?" she asked his mind, hoping to trick him into thinking of its whereabouts. More singing and various images of his house, his friends, his dog, his truck, and his yard. They had searched the house, truck, and yard, a dozen times already and had found nothing. They knew Council didn't have it, so it had to be hidden elsewhere or at his Allies house.

"Give me the location of the moonstone, or we'll kill your Allies." She said to his mind again. At once, she was bombarded with images. It meant nothing to her, other than he was still fighting her by filling his mind with foolish imagery.

"Stop your resisting." She urged him and once again was bombarded with science fiction scenes with spacemen valiantly fighting some relentless half-robot creatures.

She dug deeper into his mind, deeper and deeper, trying to bypass all the trivial nonsense he was pummeling her with. She suddenly found herself in a misty place, a fog filled clearing with a chest-height stone sitting in the middle of it. Was this the moonstone? It didn't seem to be. The movie scenes and music were gone now, and it was silent. She walked towards the big rock and suddenly felt herself being watched... and hunted. She had ventured too far and was approaching Lord DeRom's dormant mind. She pulled back just in the nick of time, feeling his consciousness rushing towards her, roaring in rage.

She leapt back physically from the surprise of it all and smashed into a tray of medical instruments, sending them flying and her sprawling. Her heart was racing and she shook her head, regaining her grip with reality. He had almost gotten her that time. She had managed to get away again, but he had gotten closer than ever before that time. She had gone too deep and had almost let herself get caught by Lord DeRom. She'd have to be much more careful.

Once she got to her feet and checked his line again, she picked up the medical equipment that had gotten knocked all over the place. Her mind felt strange and her stomach was quivering from the excitement. She couldn't feel true fear, she just didn't have it in her, but she did feel surprised, and was now hyper-alert. Even in the state he was in now, he could destroy her with ease. If he was fit and well, he could reach his mind out and destroy her entire pack. She would need to be more cautious next time. She reinserted his IV tube, increased the alcohol feed, and waited.

****

Falcon and Natasha were making out in the barn when I found them. I jumped in surprise at the sight, then giggled and spied on them.

"I think I love you," Falcon said to her softly. Love was a new emotion for him. He had always been around vampires his whole life, and according to his people, the vampires were a male-only race. Females were of zero importance, only things to have sex with, trade for goods, or feed upon if times were tough. He had never really even spoke to many females before, and none of them were like Natasha.

Natasha smiled and then kissed him on the forehead. "I think I love you too." She said softly. "I told myself that I hated vampires, even though I am half one... but I do sincerely think that I love you too."

"I never knew your father personally, but I did hear about him. He was before my time." Falcon said. "He belonged to the Rucsor clan, didn't he?"

Natasha nodded. "Yes. Harko of the Rucsor. He was one of their enforcers, not an actual assassin though. He was too brutish for that." She told him. Falcon had met dozens of enforcers who were too brutish to be an assassin. An assassin had to have tact, grace, and be smart. The enforcers were little more than bullies and thugs, used as soldiers and guards. Harko had been one of the Rucsor's head enforcers, the chief one, and his brutality and cruelty were second to none.

"I killed him." She said and Falcon nodded.

"I heard he was killed by his "drobishskii," he said to her and she nodded. I wasn't sure what the word meant, but I thought it meant daughter.

"Yeah..." she said softly. "I did it."

"How long were you your father's drobishskii?" he asked her. Apparently, it *didn't* mean daughter, but I was nearly certain it did. I knew "Drobish" meant "female offspring." I had no clue what the "Skii" part meant.

"The typical period, from my thirteenth birthday, but I killed him when I was eighteen and had met my birth mother for the first time. He had told me she was dead. Mother convinced me to kill him and then got me into the Grand Alliance just before she died, and shortly after, I met Jackette. Don't tell them I was his drobishskii for that long. I told them that my mother raised me. Humans don't see it the same way as our people do." Natasha said to him, her tone almost pleading.

He comforted her. "I won't tell them. I swear it. But, didn't the DeRom know?" he asked her and she nodded.

"Yes, he knew. I went to explain things out to him the next day, but he already knew. He knew I was Harko's drobishskii and he knew I had lied about it to Jackette and her family. He also knew why. I have been treated fairly by the Sons... and the DeRom. Very fairly. And I think of Jackette and her mother like the family I never had. I am scared of being around her father, though... he never said or did anything improper to me, but I am scared I might do something to him. I was a skii for a long time... it is hard for me to resist doing something improper to him, especially since I live with him in his house."

I wondered what she meant. Was she planning on hurting my Dad? Why? And what the hell did "Skii" mean in the vampire language? She had lied to us about her past. She had been raised by her vampire Father, not her Son Allied Mother like, she said. But Lord DeRom had known, and if he knew, I didn't care. We all had stuff in our pasts that we would rather not tell others. I couldn't blame her for that. I would, however, kick her ass if she had thought about hurting my father.

Falcon looked at her sexily. He was a damn good-looking guy in his human form, once he got cleaned up. Needed a haircut, and he was still too skinny, but Mom was fixing that.

"And what are you tempted to do to him exactly?" He said to her and she grinned and then kissed him. A few seconds later, they were both naked there in the hay.

"You can be my Skii if you want." He said to her jokingly as he rammed inside of her from behind. She gasped at him entering her and then looked insulted. "I won't be anybody's whore ever again!" she said, her voice filled with hurt. "But I will be your girlfriend if you don't already have one."

My eyes were wide as I watched them. Skii meant whore! She was her father's personal whore for the majority of her teen years? I don't know what shocked me more, the fact that she had done that or the fact that she had wanted to have sex with my Dad. If she had asked for it and he had refused, he must be the strongest-willed human male alive.

"I don't have a girlfriend," Falcon told her. I immediately

thought of the girl I had seen him with back in the cave that had given him head. "I used to have a Skii, though, but she is dead. She was killed when the Sisters took our cave from us."

"So it has been a while for you as well?" Natasha asked him as he attended her.

"Yes! Weeks! I thought I was going to explode!" He said with enthusiasm as he rammed against her happily.

"Well, it won't be weeks for either of us now!" she gasped back happily. I decided to leave them alone before I got caught spying. I didn't know whether to laugh or cry.

I slowly backed away and snuck out of the barn without getting noticed by them. I was embarrassed by what I had seen and my heart was racing from what I had learned about my friend. I wouldn't ever say anything to her about it. She had done what she thought was right. She was still my friend and I couldn't care less what she had done in the past... even though it was disgusting. As long as she kept her hands off of my Dad. I was happy she and Falcon were together now. They made a good couple.

I went back in the house and Mom looked at me. "Where's Natasha and Falcon?" She asked.

"They are in the barn," I told her. She looked at me strangely.

"Well what are you doing in here? Why aren't you giving

them a hand?" she asked me. I burst out laughing.

"I don't think they want any help," I said to her and she looked at me oddly then the lights came on. She gasped and I nodded and she burst out laughing as well.

"Well, you had better not go help them then!" she said at last, sending us both into more fits of laughter.

Karl walked in then and looked at us. "What's so funny?" he asked and Mom and I just shook our heads. He rolled his eyes as he turned and went back into the living room.

Chapter Twelve
Loose Ends

Esau Taxiss sat in his yacht reading reports. He was an elderly man in his late seventies with silver-grey hair. He was in good shape for his age, not surprisingly, considering he never did a hard day's work in his life. He stood about five foot six and weighed about a hundred sixty pounds, not a really tall or large man, but he carried himself with authority and almost strutted as opposed to walked. He had small round glasses perched over a large hawkish nose, and his old grey eyes stared out from his round spectacles with the piercing gaze common among men who were accustomed to getting what they wanted… or psychopaths.

Six bikini-clad supermodel-looking girls in their early twenties lounged around the room, three sets of identical twins. Two redheads, two blondes, and two raven-haired, all of them vampires in their human forms. They also did whatever Esau asked of them, either to him or to each other. He had paid good money for the two redheads and the two raven-haired females that he purchased from other vampire families, the two blondes were of his own line.

Esau liked to surround himself with beauty as proof of his authority. On the floor, between the Italian handmade leather couches with the girls and his fifty thousand dollar desk, lay a fur rug of unusual shape. It was the hide of a Son, a few hundred years old when 'werewolves' were the typical full moon prowling beasts from ancient history. This one was a low blood from that era that his forefathers had managed to kill. It didn't have mental abilities and had been locked in form, so they had been able to skin it without having it turn human again.

There were said to be a few other rugs like this in existence… but most were centuries old. The Alliance had managed to clean up the bloodlines years ago, and the Sons weeded out all of the low-blooded shifters, so there were almost no more being born. Bloodlines were more carefully monitored to make sure no more low bloods were born, but it was a constant battle. Humans were promiscuous, and bastards were common.

That rug had seen much. His rise to power to become head of the entire Taxiss clan that had been made public in this very room, as well as the deflowering of hundreds of young girls on its furry back, that rug had been around for a lot of interesting times.

The old vampire set his reports down and stared out the window at the lights along the Jamaican shoreline a few hundred yards away. He was docked off of Dolphin Cove, a popular tourist area that was also a good area to avoid foul weather, and he would often moor here so he could be close to the protective coast, as well as so he could get his packages of heroin quickly delivered from the shoreline without drawing too much attention.

The heroin was just a supplement to his wealth. He had dozens of drug operations throughout the Caribbean; just one of many locales around the world working and refining the toxins so he could deliver it to his people in North America and Europe on his travels. Normally, he never took part in such lowly transgressions such as drug dealing, but his own stocks of the foul drug were getting low and he needed more and more of it to keep the bulk of his subordinates in line. Junkies were much easier to control, and they worked relatively well as long as they knew they could get more of the drug. It would cost more to keep them under his thumb, but it was a cost, he had recently learned, that was well worth it.

He could not afford another rebellion amongst his underlings. The last one had cost him several million dollars and numerous lives. He could care less about the lives truthfully, but it did make him look weak in the eyes of the other vampire Lords. If he looked weak for any amount of time, they might decide to take what was his, and that would not be good. But he would soon look far from weak. Reports were coming in now that the Sisters of Slaughter had all but abandoned his former fortress and so he sent the bulk of his forces there to take it back. Taking it from another vampire family looked good; taking it back from someone like the Sisters of Slaughter would make him downright famous… even if there was only one or two of them there.

A large vampire male wearing a black suit, mirrored

sunglasses, and black leather gloves came into the room, a submachine gun slung over one shoulder. Esau looked at him curiously.

"Master Taxiss. I need a word with you. Permission to lock down?" He asked nervously and then spoke into a radio microphone on his collar once Esau nodded. At once, steel doors slid down over all the windows and the doors locked. The entire room was impenetrable now. It was even waterproof and detachable in case the boat sank. More importantly, it also made it soundproof to any prying ears of drug enforcement officials.

Esau looked at his guard, Braco. The large male looked at the six girls and disregarded them. They were nothing. "Did you speak to the Son Emperor's people yet? Are they angry with us? Did they say anything to make you think that they are on to our plan to retake our home?"

"They care nothing about it. I spoke to the Emperor's people myself this very day. I expressed our desire to maintain peace with the Sons and acted as if I did not know that their Emperor had been slain. They, too acted as if nothing was wrong, and they seemed to act like he was still alive. I didn't let them know that I knew he had passed." Esau said. "Also, his allies say that the Sisters are rebels, I was told, working freelance as we had long suspected. They say that we can expect no repercussions from the Sons if we slay them. I believe they would even be pleased if we did."

"Do you think it is a lie? Maybe his people knew you were lying to them and lied to you in return." Braco said. He was very nervous regarding doing this tricky work.

Esau thought for a moment, then shook his head. "No. I think the Emperor's people wouldn't bother lying to me if they knew the truth. They say they don't care if we fight the Sisters or if we retake our property and that suits me fine. I added that we, too, wanted peaceful relations with their kind. Once we take control of the Sisters leader, take back our home, and recover the helmet and this artifact they are after, I will make them teach us how to use their technology. They will do whatever I ask once I have her."

Braco nodded. "We DO want peaceful relations with his kind!" he thought frantically. He had seen the Sisters in action, and eight of them had butchered almost a hundred of his crack troops in a matter of minutes without suffering a single loss. They could get into your head somehow, control your thoughts and make you turn on your friends or even yourself. They could even turn invisible if there were more than one of them. Their technology would only make them stronger. He wanted no fight with them at all, if possible.

"The Sisters have the helmet, and they have gone to Canada. The Sisters leader however is unguarded and alone in our fortress for some reason. I suspect they are using the helmet to make a move on Lord DeRom's grounds in Canada to claim his portal and get the artifact they are after, so while they are active there, we will retake our home and the head bitch with it." Esau said with satisfaction. All the pieces had fallen into place perfectly so far. He had no reason to think they wouldn't continue going into place now.

Braco nodded in understanding, but felt scared. This whole thing depended on getting the fortress back, capturing the head Sister, threaten to kill her if the other Sister's didn't obey, and then getting her to show how to use the helmet and this artifact to open portals. He didn't have faith that it could be done, even with there only being one Sister at the fort. It was a risk his Master was willing to take, but he would rather not.

Esau looked at Braco and spoke, his old voice cool and collected. "The Sisters are likely moving against the DeRom grounds to search it. The portal he has on his grounds is among the strongest natural portals in existence. They say that with the proper vibrational energy, you can travel anywhere on Earth… and even possibly through time itself. It's the reason the DeRom settled in that region in the first place. Now that they have the helmet and the Emperor is dead, they are after the artifact he was recently given. We have people near to his location and they tell me that there are several people staying at his Ally's house. They are preparing for an attack there. We are safe."

"So they do not care that we are planning to attack the fortress? What if there are more than one of them there?" Braco asked.

Esau smiled. "We have the advantage in numbers. I am not worried. They are an ocean away and their forces are divided."

"Well I am worried." The guard said nervously. His Master hadn't fought the Sisters in hand-to-hand combat, he had. Even one was to be feared. He was lucky to have made it out of their fortress alive. Many hadn't.

Esau was about to reply when the radio on Braco's collar blared. All he could hear was machine guns and screaming from the other end.

"COME IN! COME IN! SAY AGAIN?" Braco roared into the microphone but nothing came back. All that he could hear was guns firing and screaming, punctuated by the odd roar. Son roars.

"They didn't stay on the DeRom grounds! They used his portal to come here!" Braco screamed at his master.

"They can't! It's impossible! They cannot portal to a moving or floating object! Radar would have detected another boat!" Esau screamed back.

Eventually, it grew quiet. Braco crouched behind the desk for cover, but Esau just paced around the room angrily, holding a perfectly preserved German Luger from World War Two. His father had taken the gun from a Nazi he had killed during the battle of Stalingrad, and it had been given to Esau by his father when Esau became the leader of the Taxiss family.

The boat eventually grew quiet, the bulk of his forces now dead, and everyone in the control room butchered where they stood. Braco and Esau eventually heard nothing but static from the radio now on every channel they tried. Everyone on the boat was likely dead now, except for them. It had only taken a few minutes.

"How's that possible! They can't portal to here!" Esau said fearfully, turning to stare at the rug nervously.

"Well, they can still fucking swim! You put us too close to shore!" Braco accused Esau, who only stared at the old rug and clutched his Luger with shaking hands.

Esau went over to Braco and yelled into the radio on his guard's collar. "This is Esau Taxiss! What do you want?" he yelled to the intruders. He was certain they could hear him.

A moment later, a voice ripped into his mind, into everyone's mind on the ship. "We want to destroy you. You will soon be no longer a threat to us." The voice said. It was one of the Sisters, he couldn't tell which.

Esau looked at Braco and then grimaced in pain. A pain was

shooting through his head like someone stabbing him in the eyes with a hat pin. He fell to the ground, clutching his skull. He felt blood coming out of his nose and ears.

"He's having a stroke!" Braco yelled at the bimbos, who just looked around stupidly. They didn't even know how to read, let alone treat a stroke victim. They were only ever used for sex. They didn't know much about anything else.

Braco laid his master down on the fur rug and tried to comfort him, then he too suddenly gasped in agony as he felt the same agony Esau had felt course through his eyeballs. He heard the girls begin screaming too, as they began rolling around on the floor in agony, clutching their heads.

He struggled to his feet and made it to his Master's desk. He hit a button on the keyboard of the computer and immediately the computer screen on the desk flicked over to their worldwide messaging system. "We are under attack! Sisters of Slaughter! I Repeat! We are…"

He fell back into the chair then, his eyes, nose, and ears gushing blood and he fought to stay conscious, the pain in his head utterly exquisite with its savagery. He had heard they could get into your head with their minds, he had felt it before, but this time, it was a thousand times stronger. The face of one of the guards from another fortress in the Middle East flicked onto the screen.

"Lord Taxiss? Could you repeat your last message?" the vampire on the other end asked casually before noticing the blood-pouring face of Braco staring back at him. He gasped in surprise and asked Braco what had happened, but it was too late for the guard to answer. He was too far gone now to say anything coherent.

The vampire on the other end just watched Braco in horror as he clawed out his own eyes and then died in a bloody heap right on top of Esau's desk. He could hear nothing but the six screaming girls, and then slowly, they too grew quiet.

He watched for a few more minutes until the screen on Esau's end had timed out and flicked off, but just before it did, he thought he had heard roaring come from the other end of the line, and then he noticed that he had a bloody nose.

****

"Where is the moonstone? We need to make sure it is safe. You have to tell me where it is!" She purred into his mind with soothing, trusting tones. She was getting mad at him and his infernal imagery and music. Everything she asked him, he'd answer with singing, taunts, or ridiculous imagery. All she got this time was more random images and laughter.

She had to go deeper into his mind, but it was desperately dangerous for her to go too deep. She had to push the Host's consciousness right to the brink and use him to get the information from Lord DeRom himself. She wouldn't dare go deeper to get it from Lord DeRom herself. Even with his Host drugged, Brav'Dos' mind was far too powerful for her to confront directly.

"Go back. Go way back into your mind. Go back to the beginning when the moonstone first came into your possession." She asked his mind. She could feel him struggling to fill her head with nonsense and music again, but she did get an image in her head of a wrapped package being handed to him by a young man in a blue suit. The man in the suit looked to be a courier of some kind.

She pushed deeper then, struggling to learn more. She was perched right on top of the bed with him, squatting on top of him, clutching his head with her hands. "Show me more." She purred to him and she finally seen the moonstone, being held by human hands this time. It was a small, round crystal and it was no more than the size of a small plum. She had found out that it had come from the moon of the O'Sian home world eons ago. It was a stone that was older than Earth's star, and it was sitting right there in front of her. It looked so real right now that she actually tried to grab it and almost fell off the bed. She could have sworn that she actually felt it.

The image faded and the incessant singing came back in her head as she lost her focus. She redoubled her efforts to get back to where she was previously inside his mind, but failed. She cursed her stupidity at having reached for something that wasn't actually there, but she had learned more than she ever had this time, so she couldn't be too upset with herself. She now knew what it looked like, at least. He was beginning to break. It was only just a matter of time now. Just a matter of time.

Chapter Thirteen
The Kerfuffle

Falcon and Natasha had come out of the barn a while later, looking happy. They were holding hands, and I smiled at them as they came inside. They saw that I noticed the hand holding and they smiled at me.

"Come on in. I was just about to go. Suppers ready." I told them. Falcon's sky-blue eyes lit up and he smiled and went inside immediately. Natasha and I stayed at the doorway.

"So... are you two a couple now?" I asked her and she just grinned and then nodded. "That's awesome!" I told her and then hugged her. I was happy for her. I was happy for them both. "You know, you're the best friend I ever had." She said to me. I told her the same.

We let go of each other and went into the kitchen. The vampires were all sitting at the table, plates heaped, just waiting for everyone else to sit and join in. They were very polite, which surprised me somewhat, and devoutly religious. Every meal was prayed over, and they refused to eat unless everyone else was ready to begin as well. I thought it was sort of strange, the whole religious vampire thing. I could only imagine the look on their victim's faces before they were ready to bite into someone's neck and drink their blood they started off by saying, "Bless me Father, for this meal which I am about to receive."

Our meal finished and the vampire men immediately got up and began cleaning the table so Mom wouldn't have to do it. Karl and Mike monitored their scanners for any indication that anyone was around and Dad, Natasha, Mom, and I went into the living room to watch television since we weren't allowed to help clean up. For notorious male chauvinists, they sure babied us.

An hour later, Mike leapt to his feet and went to the window. He had his scanner pointed out towards the blackness outside through the glass and he stared at it intently. A second later, Karl's scanner at the opposite end of the house began beeping and he ran over to it, fingering his weapon. "Take your meds!" he roared to everyone and everybody ran to this large bag to get the pills they had told us about a few days ago. They were made of some drug that negated the effects of some of the Son mind techniques, but they hadn't been thoroughly tested yet. We weren't sure they would work on the vampires if they shifted, but Karl was fairly certain they would work if they remained in human form. They decided to stay in human form rather than risk having a Son take control of them.

Dad looked at us and told us to go into the cellar. Our cellar was old, just a clay basement, really, and it had one small window. We took the dogs, Laddie and Moon, down there with us and then barricaded ourselves down there in a small back room. Dad had the rifle Karl and Mike had given us, and Mom had taken the family shotgun. Natasha and I just had our butcher knives.

The vampire men each grabbed a weapon from Karl's bag and took guard beside a window. They did not look out of the windows after Karl had told them that they could be charmed or even taken mental control of if a Son was outside and made direct eye contact with him. It would be better to attack the back of anything that might come in through the glass instead of attacking it head on.

We were in the basement for a few minutes when the phone rang upstairs. I heard Karl speaking to someone and then hanging it up. A second later, he yelled down to us. "The Sisters have killed Esau Taxiss and over a hundred of his best troops in his yacht off of Jamaica."

Natasha looked at me. "Well, that's good news then! If they were in Jamaica, that means they can't be here!" she said and I shook my head in disagreement. "The portals can take them pretty much wherever they want to go in seconds," I said to her. She grimaced and then returned to the rest of us away from the door. She had forgotten about the portals.

The phone rang again and I heard Karl's deep voice answering it again. He hung up and a few seconds later, yelled down to us again, this time laughing. "Jesse loves you." He yelled and Mom rolled her eyes and Dad looked annoyed. Natasha and I both looked at each other and laughed. "Which one of us?" She yelled up to Karl after we had stopped.

"Jackette this time." He said and then shut the door to the cellar again. I could hear him laughing upstairs.

"He's persistent, I'll give him that," Dad said with a chuckle. "A complete idiot, but persistent." I just rolled my eyes and felt myself blush.

All of a sudden, I heard a strange noise and realized it was the weird weapons Karl and Mike had, firing. I heard a window smash from upstairs somewhere. I heard weapons firing and the house was filled with roaring and men yelling. We heard a scream from one of them and then more firing.

A second later, one of the Sisters came smashing down the cellar steps. Another one followed her and we could hear them in the room next to us, tearing it apart, looking for us.

The basement was full of stinky old potatoes, our winter wood, and damp earth, but the Sisters could smell us over all those other scents like we were covered in skunk spray. I could hear what sounded almost like a machine gun firing, but it was very high-pitched. Whatever was going on upstairs had everyone up there busy.

"GIVE US THE MOONSTONE OR YOU WILL ALL DIE!!" ripped into our minds all at once.

"Fuck you!" I heard Mom scream as she fired at the arm of the Sister who had just smashed through the wall next to us from the other room. They were coming through the wall instead of the barricade, which had now penned us in the room instead of protecting us.

The Sister's arm was vaporized almost right up to the elbow. She withdrew what remained with a scream of agony and a moment later, I heard more screams and yells from upstairs. It sounded like they were bouncing elephants on the kitchen floor and having a shouting match above us.

A few seconds later, it was silent. A few seconds after that, Karl was at our door, telling us they had left.

He took down the barricade and looked around at the cellar. A trail of destruction came down the stairway. They had obliterated the door coming down here, as well as the wall between our hiding area and the next little room. It didn't get any better as we went further up into the house.

"One of the vampire lads didn't fare out so well," Karl said to us as we walked into the kitchen. Natasha gasped and ran to the kitchen. It was soaked in blood and looked like a bomb had gone off inside of it. A large hole was in the wall where one of the windows had been, and the body of Silas lay in a bloody pile on top of the cupboards.

"She came directly in through the window, leapt right past Jacob, and grabbed him," Karl said as he motioned towards Silas's body. "Jacob managed to shoot her a few times, as did we all before she died, but she had already killed Silas. She's over there, or what's left to her."

We looked to where he had motioned and seen a naked woman lying on the floor by the stove. She was a big girl, in her early thirties I figured from the look of her, with jet black hair. Her body was shot to hell, with scorch marks all over her chest, back and head. Her lower half was covered in Son ritual scars, which crisscrossed large designs over her legs and back. In Son form, it would look like raised patterns of bare skin through the fur, their form of tattoos, but in human form, it looked like she had been tortured with whips or something. She more than likely hadn't been in human form in years.

"Any other ones?" Dad asked and they shook their heads.

"Eliza blew the arm off of one downstairs," Dad said and the two big men looked at her approvingly. Falcon wasn't looking at anyone other than Natasha, and Jacob was curled up in a corner sobbing hysterically.

"What do you figure they will do now?" I asked Karl and he

looked at me with a strange look on his face.

"They'll hit us again. And soon. We got one and wounded another. Lord knows how many are here. It could be that all of them came, but we can't tell."

"Can we fight them off?" Dad asked him and Karl looked at him with a doubtful look on his face.

"I doubt it. We can sure try though. They said something about the moonstone, didn't they?" he asked and I nodded.

"Yeah, they did. I heard it as clear as day from the one in the basement. I don't know much about what it is. Some artifact." I told him honestly.

"The moonstone is said to be one of the most powerful artifacts the O'Sian's created for drawing energy from the astral realm. It can take energy from there and transfer it to our realm in the form of energy for the portals or to trigger O'Sian devices, but it can also draw energy from our realm, like our soul energy, and use it to do things in the astral realm." Mike said, stopping us all in our tracks. It was the first time many of us had even heard him speak, and the most he had ever said at any given time since we had met him.

"It has the power to collect souls. It is said that it contains the souls of thousands of criminals captured by the O'Sian high priestesses long ago. It was originally a prison for pure evil... but in the wrong hands it can be a weapon of terrifying results. It was rumored to be formed from a stone from the moon around the O'Sian's home world millions of years ago. It can give power to weapons of incredible power or to supercharge the portals so they can be used to travel off world or even through time… theoretically. With the moonstone, the portals could also be weaponized to act like mini black holes all over the planet. Only a very powerful Son mind can trigger the moonstone to work though, perhaps with a Bar'Ka'Nofa helmet or a Royal DeRom."

We all stared at Mike, who just finished his spiel and then stared at us in return. "What? I studied in our temples all of my youth." He said matter-of-factly.

Karl looked at Dad curiously and the rest of us then. Dad looked back at him and spoke. "Well apparently, Rob had this moonstone thing and now the Sisters want it. If he did have it, I had never seen it. I swear it. I never heard of it before now."

Karl studied him carefully, trying to determine if he was lying to him. After a few seconds, he spoke. "We should prepare our defenses and patch up these holes. They'll be back, and soon." Dad nodded and then went back downstairs to get some lumber he had down there. A few minutes later, we heard him screaming for help.

We got down there and found him in the corner, fending off

the one-armed Sister with an axe. Karl drew his gun and fired at her, hitting her in the chest three times. She dropped in a pile, snarled, and then started to move again. He went over to her, aimed at the back of her head and fired again, finishing her off. We all watched in fascination as she reverted back to her human form in a few seconds.

"Jesus Christ, they take a beating!" Dad said, his voice shaking. He still held the axe in his hands, his knuckles turning white from his super grip.

"Yes they do," Karl said, holstering his handgun. "And they can give one too. Now let's go up there and get this place secured, and get poor Silas down off the cupboards while we're at it."

****

The head Sister crouched over Rob's prone body strapped to the hospital bed. She had ordered the Sisters of Slaughter to return to Prince Edward Island by portal after they had finished off Esau and the bulk of the higher-end Taxiss vampires, and went back to digging into Rob's mind. They had the helmet with them, which allowed them to greatly amplify their mental powers to do the bulk of the killing in Jamaica. It was proving to be a handy weapon indeed. Coupled with the moonstone, it would be the dawn of a new era… and the death of the present one.

"Tell me more about the stone. Show me more." She asked him repeatedly, delving deeper and deeper into his mind, searching for secrets. She was discovering more and more as she dug deeper and deeper, using her telepathy to unlock more and more secrets from inside his mind.

But still, he wouldn't tell her. She found herself in the mist again and proceeded with caution. She saw Rob sitting there on the rock in the middle of the foggy area, looking weak. She approached him slowly, gently, wary of any sign of Lord DeRom being nearby.

"Greetings." He said to her in a deep voice, he looked up at her and his eyes were golden. Now she was getting somewhere! She had gone into Lord DeRom's and the Host's shared unconsciousness. She had one with her Host too, some pathetic screaming girl that she had locked inside her mind ages ago. She was pretty much all herself now, with no Host mind to speak of anymore. All the Sisters were that way. All of them had disposed of their Host's ages ago. They had simply shifted into Son form and had never shifted back. Their Host's were little more than a distant memory now, a tiny, screaming mess shoved somewhere in the darker recesses of the more powerful Son mind. Little more than a minor side thought at the best of times.

"Greetings." She said back respectfully. "I seek information regarding the moonstone, Lord DeRom."

"The Moonstone is protected by the loyal grey Guardian." He said to her calmly. She nodded in reverence and then persisted delicately.

"We fear that it has fallen into the wrong hands. We need to protect it." She said to him, trying to sound panicky.

"It is safe. The grey Guardian has it." He told her sagely.

"Who is the Host of the grey Guardian?" she probed, hoping for a name. It had to be one of the Allies. If they were an Alpha or a Son, she should have heard about them before now. It had to be a carefully guarded relic, indeed. Even the Temple Priestess that guarded the most sacred relics could be communicated with mentally. They were the only group that were referred to as Guardians. This one must have been raised in private and kept isolated from the mental communication web that they all shared. It had been done before.

"The grey Guardian is a loyal friend. The grey Guardian is powerful. They cannot lose their soul to the stone." He said to her, driving her to the brink of her patience.

"Is the grey Guardian an Alpha?" she asked. He shook his head no.

"Is the grey Guardian a Son then?" she asked and he shook his head no. She was super confused now. It was either a Son or an Alpha, it couldn't be neither.

"The grey Guardian is a daughter." He said with a slight smile. She cursed under her breath. At least she learned that the grey Guardian was a female, but all temple Guardians were. Did he have a secret child with a member of one of the grey-furred families? Most of them were healers, not warriors. A royal pairing would be common knowledge, and there hadn't been one.

"Tell me more about this Guardian." She asked him but he shook his head no again. "There is nothing more to say about her." That was all he would tell her... over and over again.

"Tell me where to find the moonstone!" She said, her anger getting the best of her. He withdrew off of the rock and walked away from her. She followed him deeper into the mist, hounding him for information.

****

The Sisters hit the house again, and then again. They managed to kill another one, blasting her almost a dozen times with their energy rifles before she finally dropped, but Mike got wounded badly, as did Falcon, in the process. Jacob still remained curled up in the corner, sobbing like a maniac. I asked if he was in shock and Karl just shrugged.

"I thought he was crying over the loss of his brother at first, but I'm thinking now that it is much worse than that. He probably stared one in the eye and she got in his head. Looks like the "Dark Look," poor little bastard. Triggered his fear response to go through the roof. He'll be like that till she's either dead or he is." He replied.

I got Natasha and Mom to help me get him to the couch, out of the way of the windows. He was almost catatonic with terror and had to pretty much be carried; unable to really even walk on his own.

Karl monitored the scanners like a hawk while Natasha, Mom, and I took care of the wounded. Mike was hurt, both his legs had gotten raked by their claws really bad, and Falcon had gotten hit hard in the head by something and now had a concussion, but we figured both of them would heal in time... if they got medical help soon.

"Ok folks, the ladies are coming back! Get in here, grab a gun, then get some cover!" he yelled to us. We obeyed as fast as we could, leaving the three wounded in the pantry.

Three of the Sisters smashed through the wall of the house at once, upstairs. Karl cursed, then flung a handful of something he had in his pocket on top of the hot woodstove in the kitchen.

Whatever it was began to smoke badly and he told us all to get down on the floor. The smoke set off the fire alarms throughout the house and it billowed upstairs. A few minutes later, we could hear them roaring, leaving the upper level and going back outside.

"What the hell is that?" I asked him and he looked at me and grinned. "Stink bomb for Sons." He said and then laughed. Whatever it was, it utterly reeked, and it had worked. They were forced to get back outside but we were all left with watering eyes and running noses.

Dad started shooting all of a sudden and the barricades we had put over one of the huge holes in the wall caved in. A Sister stood there wearing some style of helmet, roaring at us and we all could feel our heads just screaming as she tried to enter our minds like they had done to the vampires on the boat in Jamaica. The drugs Karl had given us were working, though, and all we got were skull-splitting headaches.

We fired at her and she roared again angrily and then disappeared, running through the house and disappearing somewhere in the back rooms. We heard gunshots coming from Falcon and Mike in the back pantry and we rushed back to rescue them, managing to chase her off, but not before she had managed to decapitate little Jacob with one swing of her powerful hand.

Mike collapsed in a pile then, unconscious, and Karl checked him over. "He's out. Blood loss and all the strain. Falcon wasn't looking too much better, but he was still awake, sort of.

We heard another smash, this time around the back of the house, and we could hear the remaining Sisters roaming around the back rooms, searching the house.

"Give us the moonstone and you will be spared!" A voice screamed inside of our minds from one of the Sisters. "We don't have it!" I screamed out to them in Son.

"Lies! It calls to us! We know it is in this house! We know you brought it here! Give it to us or we shall decorate our hall with your hides!" the voice screamed inside of our minds again.

"I swear to you that we don't have it!" I yelled out to them in Son again, but they wouldn't listen.

The large pantry door began to shake like they were hurling themselves at it. It was one of those old heavy wooden doors, three inches thick and made of solid maritime Oak, but it was cracking. It wouldn't hold much longer. We could hear it splintering bit by bit.

Karl blasted a hole right into the snarling face of the first Son he saw coming through the crack in the pantry door. She fell backward, killed instantly, and we heard the other Sister scream at us in rage before running into the kitchen and leaving. When we got out, we discovered she had done two things.

The first thing she had done was she took Karl's sack weapons and equipment that he had left in there and thrown it all outside, which unfortunately, was almost everything. The second thing she had done? She set the house on fire.

****

Ma'Gora pursued the Host through the mist slowly. Every so often he would stop and talk to her, answering her questions with riddles and Zen-like answers, then he would wander off into the mist of his mind again. She felt she was getting closer though, so she kept hounding and hounding him. Just when she was about to give up, he'd say something slightly different.

"I will get it from you. I will follow you to the furthest reaches of your mind until you tell me where it is." She said calmly. She wasn't playing his game of getting her angry anymore. She wasn't going to fall for that trick again. As soon as she lost her temper, she'd snap back to reality and need to enter his mind all over again. She had fallen for that trick enough already and wasn't allowing herself to fall for it again. She also wasn't letting him lead her too far into the mist. That was where the bulk of Lord DeRom's unconscious mind lay, and if she went in there, he could possibly awaken from his forced dormancy even through the alcohol, and that wouldn't be good.

"Get what from me?" This time, it was the pure Host consciousness asking her the question. She had encountered several of his different consciousnesses. Everyone had them, humans too. They were little personalities we all throw around depending on the situation. Host's just tended to have a couple more. The only thing she could do would be to plough through them all one by one, calmly, until she got some information she could use.

"Oh, Just some information on the moonstone." She said to him nonchalantly. She expected him to start rambling on about grey Guardians or to start singing again. He didn't.

"What do you want to know?" he asked her calmly. She wasn't ready to expect much yet, but she figured it wouldn't hurt to ask.

"Oh, just where it is. We've been looking for it for a long time now." She said to him calmly. He just nodded.

"It's at the MacNeill farm now. My allies." He said to her simply. She just blinked.

"Where at in the MacNeill farm? Precisely?" she asked. Now, she was starting to get somewhere. Perhaps he had finally broken down and she was past all the stupid barriers he had been throwing around since they captured him.

He frowned. "Not sure. But it smells bad." He said. It was better than singing, she figured. Stinky places at a farm didn't give her much help, but it would narrow down the search a bit. The Allies there didn't seem to know what they were talking about. Whether they had learned to block their minds or truly didn't know where it was didn't really matter much. There were several truly stinky spots they needed to look in; the entire barnyard, the manure piles, or the septic tank. The last one she'd make someone else check. Wading waist-deep in human fecal matter wasn't her idea of a good time. It wouldn't be a good story to tell her subjects once she took control of this planet that she had found the moonstone after rooting through a tank of shit.

"Thank you very much!" she said to him and he just smiled. "Glad to be of assistance!" he said cheerfully in return.

"Would you be so kind as to inform me precisely where it is if you ever find out?" she asked him. He nodded enthusiastically. She must have gotten into some child region of his mind, he was willing to please and very trusting. She should have come here sooner.

"Oh-oh." He said fearfully. She looked at him.

"What's wrong?" she asked. "It's too late, you idiot!" She thought triumphantly. You already told me enough!" He was more than likely Oh-oh'ing about having realized that he had told her all she needed to know.

"You're in trouble now!" he told her in a sing-song voice. She laughed. "And why's that?" she asked him. She wasn't anywhere near Lord DeRom's region of his mind anymore and with him being forced into dormancy from the booze, she had nothing to fear if she stayed away from it. "Because you weren't supposed to tell me where the moonstone was?"

"No." He replied innocently. "Because you knocked out my alcohol feed about two hours ago."

****

We managed to put the fire out in the house, but there was now so much smoke that it made seeing anything outside all but impossible. We were now fortunate that the Sisters had blasted out so many windows and doors during their previous attacks because now smoke billowed out of them instead of choking us all to death inside.

She hadn't done much, really. She had knocked the stove pipe out of the flue and then thrown a few half-burned sticks that were in the stove out onto the floor. We managed to catch them quickly and put them out, but if we had delayed coming out of the room any longer, it would have meant our deaths.

We still had Mom and Dad's shotgun and rifle, but we were now desperately low on ammunition. Mike still had his handgun with him, as did Karl, but they said they were both D.N.A. bonded to them and that they wouldn't work for anyone other than them. That was probably a good thing because none of us had ever fired a handgun before... except Falcon, but he was content using a big energy rifle whenever his vision cleared enough for him to use it.

She had taken all the rifles the vampires were using as well, and while she had not taken Falcon's when she had attacked them in the other room, it had gotten damaged, and now only worked sporadically.

The scanners were gone as well, which proved to be the main loss. Also, the electricity was out now too, thanks to a large chain she had thrown over the power lines coming into the house, knocking them off of the pole and sending us all into the blackness with her.

We could barely see a thing outside of the house. We could hear her roaming around out there, though, messing with our minds, and trying to get us to waste ammo. It wouldn't work with the rifles Karl had brought in, but most of those were now outside with her and none of us dared make an attempt to go get them. Karl had tried and had gotten shot in the legs as soon as he set foot outside. We drug him in and stopped the bleeding, the wounds not being a fatal ones, but he was as mobile as a three-hundred-pound stone now.

I was thankful that we had those drugs that negated their mental abilities. They couldn't charm us now at least, or mask to make themselves invisible. They still managed to do the "Dark Look" though, but that seemed to be it… for now.

They tried various tactics. Every so often, a large rock would come flying inside through a window or opening, and they'd attempt coming in through the other side of the house. After they realized that we had figured out that every time they made a distraction on one side and tried coming in the other side, they began randomizing the attacks; sometimes coming in the same place they had thrown a rock, sometimes not.

Every so often, we would all get a splitting headache and we would feel them testing our limits with the Bar'Ka'Nofa helmet, seeing if the drugs were wearing off yet. The rest of the drugs were outside in the duffle bag with the rifles, and we knew that now it was just a matter of time before the ones in our systems wore off. Once that happened, it would be game over. They'd just get inside our heads and have us turn on one another, or they'd just finish what she was attempting to do now with the headaches, except once the drugs wore off, the headaches would kill us.

"Persistent bitches." Dad said as he cursed at himself for

shooting at shadows. They had chased the cows from the barn out into the yard, and were using them for moving cover now. They could also control their thoughts somewhat and every so often, several of our cows would charge at the house in a stampede and threaten to overtake us. We had to shoot several. Thankfully, we didn't have many.

Mom was out of shells now and Dad only had four rounds left. We sat in the remnants of the kitchen, our stronghold since it offered us the best views of the property, as well as allowed us access into the cellar where we would have our final stand if it came down to that.

"We need that duffle bag back," Karl said. Dad and Mom both nodded in agreement. Natasha sat in the corner, nursing Falcon and Mike. Both of them were unconscious now, Falcon lasting long enough to get moved into the kitchen once again after we abandoned the back pantry. The big door was torn to shit on it now anyways.

"The drugs are wearing off. I figure another half hour or so and they won't be working at all. After that, all the ammo and firepower in the world won't mean a lick of difference." Karl said.

We could see the duffle bag sitting out in the yard, tempting us. We all looked at it, wondering if we could make it if we tried for it. Every time one of us figured they could, they'd fire at us with one of the weapons they had stolen from it. It was filled with weapons made for Son's use, after all, and they were proving to be pretty good shots. Karl could testify to that. He had lost a lot of blood and was starting to get dopey.

"Think they'll continue if the sun comes up? It's going to be dawn soon... another hour or two." Mom asked. Karl shook his head.

"Yeah, they are going against Son law. Making an attempt on the throne. They don't give a shit for the laws now. They'll walk down the middle of Main Street at high noon now. I figure that there must be another one of them somewhere else, though."

"Can't you call the Council? Let them know what's going on?" I asked. He just looked at me and laughed.

"My ability to communicate mentally with Council is weak compared to theirs. That and the drugs negate that type of stuff. You can't have the best of both worlds. I'm very weak mentally compared to a Son. They can easily block me. The phone lines are down too, and my cell won't work either. They must have a scrambling field set up. No communications can come in or out of here now. That guy Jesse was the last person to get through, and that was just because he was local. Snuck in under the wires, but they have that sealed off tight now, too. I checked a few minutes after he called last time, just before they attacked. Nothing. Wouldn't matter anyhow, Council won't interfere with this type of thing."

"What?" I asked him incredulously. "This isn't important

enough for them or something?" I couldn't believe the Council would just stand by and let something like this occur without saying anything about it.

"This is between the DeRom, us, and the Sisters of Slaughter. It doesn't involve the Son people as a whole. None of Council's business." He said as he peered into the darkness, trying to see if the shadow he seen was from a Sister or another cow. It moo'ed and he lowered his gun.

"Well, we're going to have to get that bag, people. Who's the fastest?" he said, looking at Dad, Mom, Natasha, and myself. I told him that I was amidst shouts from the other three protesting it. I just shook my head. "I was his Aide. It's my decision and my choice to go get that bag. But it is way too heavy for me to carry it all back in time. I'll grab what I can and get back here as fast as possible. I'll try to get the drugs first, though. It's the most important thing. We need to wait until they are at the back of the house though, if we can figure out their pattern. I can be there and back before they make it around to get me if we time this right."

"We'll need a distraction... something to get them to the back of the house. They could be able to sense our thoughts with that helmet too, so as you're running for the bag, keep thinking BARN, BARN, BARN, over and over again. It might throw them off." Karl said to me. It seemed to be a sound idea, we just needed something to lure them around to the other side of the house.

****

Ma'Gora panicked as she fought to leave his mind, but found herself in the fog. She could see where she had come in from, but every time she got to it, she'd find herself back where she was, just seeing her escape route off in the distance somewhere else. She had been lured too far into his mind. He kept moving images of the rock to let her think she wasn't in as far as she was. Now she was hopelessly lost in there now and he was waking up.

"You're in trouble... big, big, trouble." The child-like version of Rob sang to her over and over again. She would have killed him if it was possible, but it wasn't. Once she got out of his mind though, she planned to put an end to him once and for all. He wasn't necessary to find the moonstone anymore, and it was far too risky to keep him alive.

"Let me out of here!" Ma'Gora roared to him but it was futile. All he would do was chant that she was in trouble and run off into the mist, giggling, taunting her to follow him. She could hear Lord DeRom's consciousness awakening as well, every so often a low deep grumbling growl emanating from the deep mist. He was coming more and more to the surface now, the effects of the alcohol slowly wearing off now that it was disconnected. If he found her mind in there, she would be mentally ripped to shreds. And with his mind, mentally was the same as physically.

She could hear the child-like consciousness of Rob off in the mist, laughing like a small child would. "Face me, you coward!" She screamed after him, not wanting to run after him, but not wanting to stay where she was anymore. She kept finding the damn rock, no matter where in the mist she went, and she couldn't get out. She had become trapped inside his mind.

****

Jesse shut off his car and got outside. It was pitch black dark in the yard with the power out, and he couldn't see the damage done to the house from his place in the laneway. He wasn't sure what he was doing here at four-thirty in the morning, but here he was.

He hoped the door was unlocked, but if it was, he figured he could still get in. He came prepared. He had condoms, duct tape, and enough Rohypnol to knock out a cow. He'd grab both of the girls, knock them out, take them outside and have his way with them. He had five witnesses back at Claude's place who would say they seen him drinking all night, then go into the back room and pass out. They did too, but what they didn't see was him pouring out the drinks and sneaking past them when they were all drunk as hell.

He was about to sneak up to the house when something moved in the blackness near him. He froze for a second, half expecting to hear a shotgun blast, but there was nothing. He waited a few more seconds, staring towards the huge shape he had seen when it moo'ed at him.

"Fucking cow." He said and sighed in relief. He was about to go up to the house when he heard something high-pitched and tinkling, like somebody dropping a string of chains or something.

He listened a bit more, then heard shotguns and rifles going off from the other side of the house. He cursed and then ran back to his car. He had just gotten inside of it when something big scrambled over his hood. He screamed in fright and thought he seen a werewolf with a salad bowl on its head looking at him, and the next thing he remembered, he was driving down the road two miles away.

"What?" he thought wildly as he pulled the car over. The hood was covered in scratch marks and dents and he realized that he had no memory of leaving the farmhouse.

He stood beside his car, shaking. He couldn't have seen what he thought he had seen. He must have hit a dog or something, though... that was it. He thought frantically, wondering if he was having some kind of drug flashback. He stood there, then looked up at the dark sky. "God... I'm seriously fucked up." He said sadly as he started to come back to his senses.

"Give me the strength to quit the dope and the booze. I promise I won't hurt the girls. Just let me know what I should do." He said and then got inside his car. He looked at the Rohypnol lying on the seat beside the duct tape and he grabbed it and threw it out the window. No more of that kind of thinking. He'd go back home, call Cheryl, and apologize to her. Maybe if he got back with her, he could get some of himself back. He just wanted to forget all about Jackette and Natasha. He'd stop by tomorrow and apologize to them, then he'd sign up for Narcotics Anonymous and Alcoholics Anonymous, and then he'd go see Cheryl and ask her to take him back.

He started the car and drove away then, driving off into the darkness towards his mother's house in Summerside where he lived… and hopefully, a brighter future.

****

I ran as hard and as fast as I could to the bag and reached it safely. I dug through it, knowing that it would be impossible for me to carry the whole thing back. Karl had a difficult enough time carrying it in himself, and he was probably five times stronger than I was. I couldn't even budge it.

"Barn! Barn! Barn! Barn!" I kept thinking as I fumbled through the bag, looking for the small packet of white capsules Karl had left in there for us to use. The annoying thing was that they were originally in his pocket and he had taken them *out* of his pocket and put them in the bag of weapons for us all to get access to.

I had a small L.E.D. flashlight in my hand, keeping it in the bag so I could search. I trembled with fear as I expected to hear a roar and then have one of them kill me at any second, but the shots were still coming from the back of the house and I knew I might still have a few more seconds of safety left. I watched as Jesse had pulled into the laneway, drawing the Sister's attention to him at the back of the house, and then left again. I just hoped it would give me enough time.

I spied the packet under a rifle butt and pulled it out. I grabbed another rifle and was reaching for another one when I heard Natasha yell for me to get back. I was halfway back to the house when I saw the Sister charging at me out of the darkness. I didn't have a prayer of racing her to the house. I flung the drugs towards the house, praying that they would make it inside, then I spun around with the rifle to shoot her, but it was too late.

She crashed into me at full speed, sending me sprawling and knocking the wind out of me. I landed ten feet away and slid another five on my face in the cold grass. I fought to gain my wits and get up, but I was paralyzed from having the wind knocked out of me and couldn't even move.

I saw her bounding towards me, then she grasped me by the hair cruelly. She lifted me right up in the air by my hair and then roared in my face. I waited for the death blow to come, but it didn't.

"Give me the moonstone or I'll kill the girl!" she screamed at them in the house. I could hear Natasha, Mom, and Dad in there crying for her not to.

She dragged me off towards the laneway, out of sight of the house. She straddled me, pinning my hands to the ground. She stared into my eyes, her own eyes glowing a dull red, and I could feel her forcing her way into my mind. I was never so terrified in my life.

I did everything I could possibly think of to block her, but it was useless. The drugs in my system had pretty much worn off and I was under her power now. She read my mind like reading a newspaper.

"You truly do not know where the moonstone is." She said, her voice now calm.

"I told you we do not know!" I said back to her. She just

huffed.

"You were his Aide. He taught you how to hide the truth from us." She said angrily. I shook my head.

"I'm only a low-generation Ally, I can't do that yet! I'm not strong enough!" I cried. She glared at me then ripped into my mind again, probing, and tearing out everything she wanted to learn from me. I felt my nose bleed and could hear my heart throbbing in my ears. She raped my mind, taking out every memory and thought I had and examining it.

She left me on the ground then. "Stay and be quiet." She commanded like one would command a dog and I found myself unable to move from where I was at. I could only sit there on the ground, bawling my eyes out as I watched her sneaking up to the house again. I couldn't even scream or yell at them to let them know I was still alive.

She crawled up the side of it, onto the roof, and then made her way towards the chimney. She had something in her hand, I wasn't sure what but it looked like a sack, and she stuffed it inside the chimney. A few minutes later smoke was coming out of the windows of the house again.

I watched helplessly as she leapt off of the roof, a good twenty feet, and landed on her feet expertly. She then ran around the side of the house and a few seconds later, I heard her opening fire on the house with her rifle.

Shots fired back at her, and I prayed that they got her, but a few seconds later, she was coming back, alive and well, this time carrying the duffle bag full of weapons with her.

"I just shot your mother." She said coldly and then laughed at me. I could only just sit there where she had commanded me to sit, blubbering like a fool, staring at her fearfully.

"Unfortunately it was the last of my weapons power. I didn't kill her. Can you say, "That's too bad, Karakka V'Lin?""

"That's too bad, Karakka V'Lin." I heard myself say. She laughed, then ran away again, this time with a fully charged rifle. Anyone she shot with that one would die instantly. Thankfully they didn't seem to hold their charges overly long and got weaker the more they emptied. They used rechargeable battery packs similar to what rechargeable tools took, except they looked a bit larger. There wasn't many left in the bag that I could see.

I was sitting on the ground sobbing when I heard someone approaching me from behind. It was a Son, I could tell from the breathing, but I couldn't turn around to look. I sat there with my eyes closed, waiting to die, but the death blow never came. "It must be the other Sister, they said they thought there was another one or two out here somewhere." I thought.

A few seconds later, I seen Karakka V'Lin run around the house, firing at the side of it randomly, then came running back around to try to sneak in the unprotected side. She came back and looked behind me at the Son that was there behind me.

"Tra'Gor, I have them pinned down inside... but they are medicated and cannot be mentally affected. This one, however, is under my control. If you get close enough, you can break through the drug's interference. You should be able to get at them with the helmet's help soon." She said to the Son behind me. I heard a low growl and then some movement. A second later, she came into view.

"How many have we lost? How many have we killed?" I heard the new Sister say to the one that had been plaguing the house. She was the one wearing the helmet.

"Gorego is around back distracting them and then us two. As for them, I'm not sure. Two vampires at least, if not three, and possibly two Dark Angels, but I have wounded another human female and there is only a human-vampire female hybrid and a human male left in there. We will take them out easily now that we have their weapons. This one has verified to me that the drug is wearing off. I was able to enter her mind myself."

"We will not get the moonstone." The Sister named Tra'Gor, who was wearing the helmet, said. Karakka looked at her curiously.

"Why not? We know it is in this house. We only need to

finish them off and search for it. Surely, we can find it once the grey Guardian is dead. It has to be one of the females, I assumed it was either this one or the mother, but after I probed this one's mind, I realized it has to be the mother. It makes sense. The mother is the most senior of his allies. She must be the grey Guardian. Once she is dead, the stone should offer itself up to us to be found. Why do you think we will not find it?"

"Because I do not wish it to be found, and because the mother is not the grey Guardian." The helmet-wearing Sister said. She then levelled her rifle at Karakka and fired it, blasting her head like a sledge hammer hitting a melon.

I stared in disbelief at what I had just seen. Was this some weird Son betrayal? Would the last Sister let us go? What had changed their mind? Had Council finally got off their asses and threatened to wipe them out or something? Were reinforcements on the way?

I watched as the Sister with the helmet closed her eyes and focused and then I heard a sudden roar of another Sister screaming in agony around the other side of the house. Then she set the rifle down and then took a few paces towards the house which brought her into my view. I watched in an odd blend of happy horror as she bent down and picked up a broken stick and then shoved it deeply into each eye, gouging them out. Once her eyes were nothing but smashed jelly, she began shoving the jagged part of the stick into the side of her neck, twisting it in deeper and deeper until blood was spraying all over the place. She collapsed on the ground then, blood coming out of her everywhere, it seemed, while her hand still twisted the stick in deeper and deeper until the last of the life had left her.

I got up then, my body freed of the mind control since Karakka V'Lin had bit the dust and looked around. No one else was there, aside from a few remaining cows eating grass off the lawn in the gloomy predawn light.

I ran to the house, yelling that it was over and screaming for Mom. I found her, lying on the floor, with Dad and Natasha hovering over her attentively. She looked up at me and smiled weakly.

"What happened?" they asked me and I told them what had occurred. I didn't know what was going on any more than they did, but I wasn't arguing.

Chapter Fourteen
Conclusion

The portal opened and Lord DeRom exited it and looked around. His Host's house was boarded up and dark and he smelled smoke and burned beef coming from his Ally's place. He stretched his back and walked around the yard a bit. It felt good to move. His muscles were stiff and he could use a good run, but it was nearly dawn now and he didn't have the time.

He went to his woods just across the field and lay down on the soft cold ground. He willed himself to shift then, allowing his Host's mind to come forward slowly as the body was changing back to human form. He spared the Host the brunt of the pain, as always, aware that the Host's body simply could not withstand it. He let him slowly come forward as he himself regressed, until eventually, all that remained was the human body and the human mind while he wandered through the mist and past his rock, linking his and his Host's mind in the astral realm.

Rob lay there on the ground, exhausted and feeling like his entire body was frozen and burning at the same time. The pain was too much to even allow him to move a muscle, but it was subsiding like a receding tide. A few minutes later, it was gone enough to allow him to blink and scream, and a few minutes after that, he managed to get to his feet.

He found a change of clothes in a black plastic bag under a tree where he usually kept it, but a mouse had gotten into the bag and chewed holes in everything, leaving everything wet and mouldy and covered in holes. It had been there for over two months, after all.

He didn't care, though. His spare house key was still in his pocket and he walked slowly back to the house and went inside, the pain was pretty much gone now and feeing only cold, wet, stiff and mightily hung over. He tried both his cellphone and the landline, but they were both dead. He also tried the lights, but the power was off. He cursed then and made his way upstairs to his bedroom and collapsed on the bare mattress, stopping long enough to cover himself with an old blanket that had been lying over his dresser to protect it from dust.

The next morning, he awoke and stretched. He was still sore, incredibly so, but it wasn't solely from the shift. He had been tied to a bed, unable to move for over two months, and his muscles had atrophied some. "A few days of moving around and a belly full of good food and I'll be as right as rain." he said to himself.

Lying in the bed the next morning, trying to drum up enough energy to move through the cold pain and stiffness, he stopped and listened. Silence. The house was as quiet as a tomb. The big grandfather clock wasn't ticking since it hadn't been wound in months, the power was shut off, so there wasn't the usual low background hum of electricity, and the furnace was off, which usually had the pipes creaking and groaning as it circulated water through the radiators. It felt downright weird being in a silent house. It was like it had died since he had been gone or something.

He got out of bed and inspected the clothes he had come home in. He peeled them off and then went to his closet and found nothing, so he reluctantly put the musty-smelling outfit back on. He wanted to have a shower, but with no power, it was impossible. He'd have to go over to Steve's later on and get him to give him a hand getting the house up and running again.

He cleaned himself up as best he could with no water, then went downstairs and looked for something to eat. He was starving, but couldn't find a thing. His cupboards were empty, as were his fridge and freezer. That would have to be remedied as well today.

Fishing through the downstairs closet, he found an old pair of work boots and put them on, then hunted for an old coat. It was early December now, and it was cool outside. He was still cold from last night, shifting out there on the cold ground and then sleeping in wet clothes without a decent blanket in an unheated house. He would find an old coat of some sort in one of the outside sheds, though he was sure of it.

Thankfully, they hadn't cleaned out the sheds yet, and he did find an old coat in one of them. They had only emptied the house it seemed, mostly just of his food supplies and shut off his power. A trip to the store and a few hours on the phone to the power company and he'd be good to go. He looked outside, hoping to see his truck, but found it missing as well. He'd have to walk.

He made good time going over to Steve and Eliza's place, considering how he felt. He was somewhat surprised to see a cow strolling down the road, halfway between his place and theirs. He chased the cow until it made its way back towards the MacNeill home, then continued along his way.

He walked into the yard, noticing two dead naked women lying on the ground by the laneway. One of them had the complete upper half of her head missing, and the other one was a bloody eyeless mess with a stick sticking out of her neck under what appeared to be a metal salad bowl with crystals and small electrical devices stuck to it. He looked down at her for a moment, studying her, then stepped over her and made his way to the door. He was about to knock when he noticed the door was open... and lying on the ground next to a dead cow. He stepped inside through the hole in the wall where the door had previously been and looked around at the destruction. They had surely put up a helluva fight... but no matter who had gotten the best of whom, it looked like the house had lost.

He followed the destruction throughout the front porch and heard Moon whining in the cellar with Laddie. He climbed down there and patted Moon for a bit, glad to see her alive and well, then he climbed back out of the cellar after heaving her and Laddie up to the first floor. The cellar stairs were destroyed, and beside it was another dead naked woman missing an arm and riddled with holes and energy bolt burn marks. She was a big sturdy girl, maybe thirty years old, with short black hair and little fat. She wasn't cute in the anorexic Hollywood sense, but she would have been a relatively attractive girl if she hadn't been ripped up so bad and covered in ritual scars.

Moon toddled off towards the kitchen, which seemed to be unusually well-lit. He walked into the room and found half of one wall torn completely off the house and lying in chunks on the grass outside, and pieces of glass and other debris scattered everywhere. Every so often, he'd find a clean spot on the floor, but most of it was dripping with blood and covered with glass, burn marks, and chunks of busted wall plaster.

He felt a presence looking at him and he turned around to see a large man lying on the floor, struggling to keep his gun aimed at him. He had been slashed across both legs and looked like a large sack of finely hammered shit.

"Who are you?" the man demanded of him. He stared at him

and then smiled. Lord DeRom had told him two Dark angels had come here to help defend his Allies. This obviously was one of them.

"I'm Rob, the Imperial Host of Lord Brav'Dos DeRom." He said to him calmly. "Who the hell are you?"

The man grew pale and shook his head. "Impossible. We disposed of Lord DeRom's body months ago." He said, unable to keep his gun trained on him any longer. Rob just stared down at him with an amused look on his face.

"About that, it was a poorly disguised imposter. Doesn't anybody actually LOOK at a body anymore? He was a grey that had been dyed white, for Pete's sake. Didn't any of my Allies identify the body?"

Karl just looked doubtful. "Steve identified you." He said, struggling to stay conscious.

"And where is Steve, is he alive?" Rob asked Karl, already knowing he was fine. Lord DeRom had told him what had happened here last night before he shifted, as well as notified Council to send a clean-up crew and some medics, preferably from the Raag'Mare family since they were the best.

Karl nodded weakly. "He's alive. All of your Allies are."

"Good!" Rob said cheerfully to Karl. "I have to go find Steve and tell him he's an idiot. Where would I find him?"

Karl motioned towards the short hallway leading to the living room. Rob nodded in thanks and then walked back there.

Everyone was asleep except those who were dead. He found Natasha and a wounded blonde haired vampire male curled up together asleep. He walked over them and discovered the other Dark Angel asleep nearby, who was also wounded badly.

He turned around then and spied a lump over in the corner. It was Jackette and her parents, using the living room drapes which had been torn off the window as a blanket. Jackette was covered in grass stains and had a black eye and large finger-shaped bruises on her arms and face. He grimaced and then looked at Eliza. She was groaning in her sleep and holding her stomach. He could smell burned flesh coming from her and deduced that she had gotten hit with an energy weapon… but she would heal. He was glad that Brav'Dos had requested the Raag'Mare. They would be coming through the portal in his yard shortly.

He stared around at everyone and felt a wave of relief go through him. He was still standing there, thanking the powers that be for sparing the lives of his closest friends, when he heard Jackette speak.

"You're alive?" She said softly, fighting to get to her feet. He turned to face her and nodded.

"You're alive?" she asked again, this time louder. Her father and mother stirred slightly then opened their eyes and stared at him in disbelief also.

"YOU'RE ALIVE!!!" Jackette screamed this time and launched herself at him. He caught her with a wince, still stiff and sore from his ordeal, and held her tight against himself. She clung to him, screaming in joy, as everyone woke up with a start and those who knew him began shouting for joy.

****

They sat outside the house in the lawn near a campfire. Several Raag'Mare Host's and Grand Allies walked around after having had treated their wounds, and an Alliance team went around disposing of evidence. The house would need some explaining, but already one of the Alliance team was working on a report about a propane explosion. There would be no official investigation, of course. That would be all taken care of.

They would need a place to stay for a while, though, and Rob had volunteered for them all to stay at his home... once, it was habitable.

"So they kidnapped you and left a dead body that looked like Lord DeRom in its place to make us think he was dead," Steve said as he stroked Eliza's head gently. He had thought he had lost her when she got shot last night and it had scared him bad.

"Yeah. They had found out about the moonstone and wanted to use it to take over the planet. They spent weeks, hell, MONTHS probing my mind, trying to get me to tell them where it was, but I wouldn't crack. They forced Brav'Dos into dormancy by intravenously feeding me alcohol, but once she was in my mind, I managed to get her to pull the feed out without noticing that she did it. By the time we let her know it was out, Brav'Dos was out of dormancy, and it was too late for her. He came out, took control of her mind, and made her kill her friends and then herself. Getting out of the bed after being strapped in it for over two months was the really tricky part." Rob said as he bit hungrily into a hamburger.

"They said the moonstone was here. We don't have it, though. I have no idea where it is. And they said Mom was the grey Guardian... is Mom some sort of Son secret agent? Is it because she has some grey hair?" I asked him curiously. Everyone else stared at him as well, waiting for an answer, including Mom who looked somewhat insulted.

He shook his head. "Nope. Baby, there is not the grey Guardian. Moon is." He said with a grin, then patted Moon on the head. He removed her collar and held it up. The moonstone was the quartz looking piece of rock that had been hanging there around her neck the entire time.

"You entrusted your DOG with a stone capable of wiping out all life on the planet!?" Karl said to him in disbelief. He seemed angry, but he didn't dare show it towards Rob.

"Yes I did. As soon as I got it, I knew I had to hide it. And she has been the loyal grey Guardian of it ever since. The moonstone is a vacuum for impurity. Evil souls are drawn to it and they get trapped within. Animals are pure souls, innocent, and are incapable of being truly evil. Because of that, they cannot lose their souls or even have them taken. There's a plus side to not having much reason... isn't there." He said, ending his statement in a baby voice as he rubbed Moon on the head playfully.

"So is the war between the Taxiss over?" Falcon asked him weakly. He was still in very bad shape but would heal, they all were told. He would be pretty much out of commission for the next month or so, though. Natasha would take good care of him.

Rob shrugged. "That depends on you, I suppose. If you want to call yourself a Taxiss again and go on a crusade to end the suffering of your people, then I'd have to say, "No, it's not over," but if you decide to leave your people and remain and be one of my Royal Allies, then I would say "Yes." Either way, the Taxiss hierarchy is in utter shambles. The Sisters wiped them out down in Jamaica. Killed Esau. Butchered an entire boat full of his best troops, too. The Taxiss will need to restructure their entire family if they want to survive, and I would imagine that the new leaders will see that the best way to do that isn't by enslaving their own people but rather by nurturing them. The other vampire families will likely be eyeing up his territory now."

"I'll stay and serve you, if you'll have me," Falcon said. Rob just nodded and gave him a handshake. Natasha grinned at Rob and then kissed Falcon on the lips.

"So the Sisters, were they evil?" Mom asked. Rob grimaced and shook his head.

"Sort of. They were, and they weren't. They intended to do good things as far as the planet is concerned, but at the same time, they intended to do bad things as well. It's all a matter of perspective, really. I mean, everyone should ask themselves, "Am I a good person who does bad things once in a while? Or am I a bad person that does good things once in a while?" Evil is all a matter of hindsight and perspective, really."

Everyone was quiet for a minute, thinking about it. Steve looked up at Rob then. "So, will I be reimbursed for damages from all this or what?" Rob just looked at him and laughed, then nodded his head.

"Yeah, don't worry about it. The Alliance will be sending you a nice fat check once they have their story for the public all figured out. This one was all our fault, buddy. We'll make it up to you."

A Raag'Mare Host came forward supporting Karl, who limped badly with a broken leg and an arm in a sling. He had one hand around the shoulders of the Ally for support and the other holding onto a makeshift crutch.

"We're heading out now. They want to take Mike in for surgery, so I'm going to tag along. I just wanted to say goodbye to you all and that it was an honor fighting by your side." Karl said to Dad and Mom with a grin.

Steve got up and shook his hand, and was followed by Falcon and Natasha. Eliza was in no shape to really move around much so she just smiled and waved weakly at him, and I just hung onto Rob and looked up at him gratefully.

"Take care Karl. You and Mike will be getting my official thanks sent to the Council. Tell them to get Falcon here some official paperwork allowing him to be a Canadian citizen. He doesn't have any official documentation I'm willing to bet."

Karl nodded in understanding, smiling, and turned to leave. Rob let him walk a few steps before calling out to him again.

"Oh yeah, and Karl?" he said to the Dark Angel, who looked back at him. "You did a great job. If you ever want to come here and join up with us Royal Allies, you just come and do it. You and Mike both are welcome to join up. Don't be a stranger, either. Come back and visit whenever you want."

The big man nodded, his eyes almost looking teary. The Raag'Mare Host led him to a waiting vehicle and left then. Pretty much everything had been done. The dead cows had been trucked away, the holes boarded up and plastic put over the cracks, and the dead Sisters piled into a black van and hauled away as well. All that remained were a few other folks cleaning up the last bits of evidence, and the people that belonged here.

They watched the van taking Karl and Mike away drive down the long laneway and disappear into the distance. They were about to turn away when they noticed a Blue Cutlass driving towards the house.

"I'll deal with this," Jackette said, but felt a hand on her shoulder. It was Falcon.

Jesse got out of the car and walked towards us. Falcon approached him. As soon as Jesse seen him coming towards him, he stopped and put his hands out defensively.

"I just came to apologize to everyone. I don't want a fight." He said to us as he stared at Falcon. The vampire stepped out of the way then, but stood at the ready, waiting for Jesse to make a stupid move or say something wrong. For the first time in his life, he didn't.

"I was a jerk to you, Jackette. I'm really sorry. You too Natasha... I deserved what you guys did to me. Took me a while to see it, but I did. Mr. and Mrs. MacNeill, I'd like to apologize to you both as well for causing you so much annoyance with me calling all the time and acting like a total dick."

He turned towards Falcon then. "Buddy, I take it that you're Natasha's man?" he asked Falcon who just nodded. Jesse stuck his hand out to him and shook Falcon's hand. "I just hope that you treat her good... 'cause buddy, trust me on this, you don't want to get her mad at ya." he said. We all chuckled at that one.

"I'll see you around, maybe. Holy crap! What happened to your house?" He said as he finally noticed the huge hole in the wall.

"A bit of an explosion. Propane tank blew." I told him and he just gawked at the mess and then turned and walked away. He got back into his car and left. Once he was gone, Falcon sat back down next to Natasha.

"Seems like an O.K. guy, believe it or not." He said and I nodded. "Yeah, he has his moments. Last night was one of them. He sure showed up in time to save our bacon. If he hadn't had showed up in time Karakka V'Lin would have caught me before I threw the meds inside. Do you think he remembers any of it?"

Dad shook his head. "Probably not. He has no clue about anything else in life, and I wouldn't expect him to have much of a clue about last night, either. And that's the way we like it." He said. Rob just laughed and then nodded in agreement.

"So what say we go get everything hooked back up at my place, get the heat on, and go get cleaned up and eat? I'd kill for a hot bath and a pizza right about now." He said to us. Everyone was in agreement.

****

That evening, we were sitting in his house chatting. Natasha and Falcon were upstairs on Rob's computer talking to one of the Grand Allies online, figuring out immigration stuff, and Rob, Mom, Dad, and I were all sitting around his kitchen table, eating pizza and chatting.

"So they disguised a grey-furred Son and made it look like you... all so we wouldn't go looking for you?" Dad said to him as Rob explained what had gone on the night he had been abducted.

"Yeah, basically. I remember hearing a knock on the door and going to answer it and then just waking up in some big vampire compound in Ireland somewhere. After I got control of Ma'Gora, the head Sister, I got her to portal here as fast as she could, but stupid me, I sent her before getting her to free me of my bonds. I would have been here earlier, but I was in pretty rough shape. Took me a while to bring Lord DeRom out enough to warn him about all the alcohol in my system and then to get him to shift so we could get back home."

"So he shifted while you were drunk? I thought that was impossible?" Mom said. We looked at him for an answer.

"It normally is. Son's livers are about an eighth the size of ours. What would give humans a slight glow would be potentially lethal for a Son. But I've been pickling my liver steadily for years now... so he has a bit of an alcohol tolerance built up. I knew there was a plus side to us running off our yearly batch of home brew!" he said with a grin, slapping Dad on the shoulder.

I just laughed and looked at him. I didn't think of him romantically anymore. He was just his good old self again, and I was happy for that. He looked back at me, his blue eyes sparkling happily, and I stared back at him and grinned. I loved him and he loved me, but it could only ever be platonically. It had to be that way… at least for now.

He had his flaws like anyone, though. He drank too much, he ate too much, and he swore too much. But he was still a good person underneath it all, a good werewolf and a good man, and I was glad to know him.

About The Author

R.S. Wells lives in Kildare on beautiful Prince Edward Island, Canada. He lives with his wife Judy, his mother Ellie, and their two crazy dogs, Hooch and Holly. He has travelled extensively throughout Canada, working in a wide variety of fields. He loves nature, fantasy and sci-fi, writing, ancient history, and having a few drinks with friends and family.

He received a Bachelor of Arts degree in 1999 from the University of Prince Edward Island and has travelled to Japan in 1998 to teach English and also to study the martial arts.

www.ingramcontent.com/pod-product-compliance
Lightning Source LLC
Chambersburg PA
CBHW041751310726
48978CB00011BB/391